SIOUX SUNRISE

a novel by
RON SCHWAB

Poor Coyote Press
PO Box 6105
Omaha, NE 68106
www.PoorCoyotePress.com

ISBN: 1-943421-05-6
ISBN-13: 978-1-943421-05-3

5-16
NAF

SIOUX SUNRISE

1

Sam Kesterson yawned sleepily and squinted as he stepped out of the little sod house. The glaring rays of the August sun streaked through the cottonwoods across the creek and proffered no relief to the scorching, parching drought. It was still—not enough breeze to even stir the fragile cottonwood leaves—and, although the sun was just rising, the heat was stifling.

"Gonna be hotter than hell again," he murmured to himself. He shook his head dejectedly and called back into the house, "We've got some water to tote, Billy. Grab the buckets, and let's get at it."

Sam, a solid-looking, barrel-chested man, stretched his arms and legs, working out the early morning stiffness as he walked down the bare, dusty path that led to the creek. The trip to the creek was less than fifty yards, but beads of sweat were already glistening on Sam's forehead and shirtless back as he knelt at the clear stream and splashed its cool contents on his bronzed, weathered face and arms.

As he stood up, shaking the droplets of water from his face and arms, he looked impatiently toward the house. "Billy, hurry up, damn it!" he called.

A boy's voice responded, "Be there in just a minute, Pa. Can't find my britches."

Brushing back his prematurely white hair, Sam scrutinized his small domain with the satisfaction of a man who had carved his own small place in the wilderness. Sam had been among the first permanent white settlers in Jefferson County, Nebraska, having brought Martha and their four small children in a heavy, bulky Conestoga wagon from Illinois to this spot, only a few miles off the Oregon Trail, after the Civil War. Billy was born less than a month after their arrival. Sam and Martha had homesteaded the quarter section where they lived and in the ten years that followed added two more adjacent quarters to their holdings. The Big K Ranch now comprised 480 acres, most of it prime, lush native grass. The ranch was small by many standards, but the land and the sixty cows that grazed it were "free and clear" as Sam frequently reminded Martha.

Sam had chosen the table of land nestled in the hills above the creek as a natural building site. The cold, clear creek, appropriately named Rock Creek for the sandstone and hard granite that formed its bed, meandered through the grass-covered hills of southern Jefferson County and provided a dependable water supply for the small farmers and ranchers of the area. The location of the home had deferred the necessity of a well, but Sam, as he had intended for several years, planned to start the slow, painstaking task of digging a well next spring. He had also promised Martha faithfully that with the coming of fall and slowing of farm and ranch work, he would commence hewing timbers for the new frame home that was to replace the Soddy. There would be no shortage of lumber for the job since the bottomlands of Rock Creek were lined with huge, towering cottonwoods. Farther up the slopes, sturdy, hard oaks thrived and waited for thinning. The brown outer walls of the sod house were starting to deteriorate and crumble. The grass that had earlier grown so luxuriously from the sod-packed roof had now browned and withered, and it was evident that strong winds would soon begin to peel the dry covering from the roof.

The austere two-room dwelling was dwarfed by an imposing, expansive barn. Neighbors had helped Sam raise the frame structure the previous fall, and the solid, white-washed building was something of a county showpiece. Martha had teased Sam good-naturedly, but with a streak of truth, about the horses living better than she did. Sam intended to remedy that soon. The lean-to hay shed and other rickety outbuildings would have to wait a few years for replacement.

Unlike some of the neighbors, Sam could withstand the devastating drought. Cash might be hard to come by for a while, but these Nebraska hills had been kind to him. It would rain again—it always did.

It was no accident that Sam Kesterson had sunk his roots in Jefferson County. Located in southeastern Nebraska adjoining the Kansas border, the county had been relatively free of Indian troubles for some years. The Pawnee, who once roamed the rolling hills, were mostly friendly and often allied with the whites against their ancestral enemies, the Sioux. A veteran Union sergeant who had fought at Bull Run, Sam had seen enough of the atrocities of war, and these green, grass-cloaked hills had offered a secure haven for Sam and his family. In fact, Sam hadn't raised a gun at another human being in the years he had resided on the Rock Creek homestead. In the late 1860s, there had been Sioux raids on farms and ranches lying north and west of the Kesterson ranch, but Sam's homestead had come through the troubled period unscathed.

Thanks largely to Major Frank North and his brother, Captain Luther North, most of Nebraska south of the Platte River remained free from Indian trouble. In 1867, Major North had been given command of a battalion of 200 Pawnee scouts. The battalion was divided into four companies of Pawnee, and Major North's younger brother, Luther, was made captain of one of the companies. They were armed with the new Spencer repeating rifles, or "seven shooters," and the Pawnee, spurred by their ancient hatred for the Sioux and Cheyenne, had pursued their old enemies with a vengeance. Although there was talk of a Sioux uprising again in the northern part of the state, especially near the Black Hills of South Dakota, there was no apprehension in the southeast. The railroad had arrived, settlements had been established, and civilization was on its way.

With the back of his hand, Sam wiped away the salty sweat that was dripping from his thick, wiry eyebrows and stinging his eyes. "Billy, will you get down here?" he yelled.

Maude, the old Jersey milk cow, bellowed in the lot outside the barn. Several horses whinnied nervously and banged against the heavy wood stalls. The hair bristled on Sam's neck and turning toward the barn, he walked cautiously back up the path.

"Red," he called, "come here, boy. Here, Red." The redbone coonhound did not respond. The arthritic old dog usually slept on a hay pile in the barn and, without fail, limped out of the barn every morning to greet Sam and Billy, his pink tongue flapping, and his long tail wagging.

Reaching the top of the slope, Sam surveyed the clearing

around the buildings. North of the barn, he spied the rust-brown patch partially camouflaged by the tall, browning switch grass. He stepped quickly toward the dog's still form but stopped short when he came upon the animal's bloody, decapitated head resting in the soft, loose dirt just outside the barn door.

Instinctively, he turned to run to the house. His mouth opened to sound a warning, but the words choked in his throat and were muffled by the crunch of bone and gristle as a feathered Sioux war axe split his skull.

2

TEN-YEAR-OLD Billy Kesterson, a skinny, blue-eyed boy with straw-colored hair and shirtless under bib overalls, stepped out of the house barefoot. He ambled slowly down the path to the creek, two tin pails dangling from his right hand, clanging noisily as he walked, his other hand thrust lackadaisically in his pocket. The tanned, freckle-faced boy stopped intermittently to kick at the fine dirt and watch the dust puff up between his toes. He quickened his pace as he neared the creek.

"Pa," he complained, "I've got the buckets. I don't know why I got to do this all the time. Sarah never does anything. She just sits in the house and writes those silly poems. Why can't she do this sometimes? Oh! Ma says breakfast is ready. Pa? Pa, where are you?"

Billy's eyes searched along the rocky creek bank for his father. Seeing no sign of him, he waded into the translucent stream and stood there for a few moments, entranced by the foamy water splashing and swirling around his calves and ankles. Abruptly the spell was broken by a round of Maude's persistent bawling, and Billy tilted the empty pails into the creek to catch the surging waters. Then he hoisted the buckets free and, barely able to cope with the heavy load, staggered to the bank and set the full pails on the ground. Catching his wind momentarily, he started up the path and called, "Pa, the buckets are full, but I can't carry—"

Billy saw the silent form of his father stretched out face down in the dirt, the back of his head a scarlet mass. His eyes widened in terror. Suddenly, a big, rough hand closed across his mouth, and he was jerked backward down the slope, breathless from the powerful arm that clamped his chest like a vice. He was dragged, kicking and struggling, into the prickly, gooseberry thicket that covered the ground between the cottonwoods on the opposite side of the creek and was pressed brutally to the rocky ground, the hand pinching his cheeks together so tightly that Billy's teeth gouged and cut the inside of his mouth.

He looked up wide-eyed at the black-bearded, long-haired form crouched over him like a grizzly bear moving in for the kill. Perspiration dripped off the man's big, twisted nose onto Billy's heaving, bare shoulders. A powerful, thickset man, at least six feet three inches tall, Bear Jenkins looked like his namesake, and his broken, rotted teeth gave him an even more menacing, animal-like appearance.

"You say one word, you little bastard, and I'll have your balls hangin' from this bush," he whispered and moved his hairy free hand eagerly toward the horn-handled Bowie knife resting in the sheath suspended from his rawhide belt. He slipped the long razor-shark "Arkansas toothpick" threateningly from the sheath. In doing so, he relaxed his grip on Billy's mouth, and Billy kicked upward with all the force he could muster, catching the man sharply in the groin with his foot. Bear doubled up in excruciating pain and gasped for breath. Billy, seeing his opportunity, squirmed free from Bear's grasp and dashed toward the creek, oblivious to the vicious gooseberry brambles slashing and tearing at his naked feet and ankles.

His escape was cut short when a squatty, brown-skinned man brandishing a Sioux war club in his right hand stepped into his path. Billy dodged to his left in an attempt to slip by the Indian. Simultaneously, the round flint head of the club arced downward, glancing off Billy's right temple before he slumped quietly to the ground.

Bear crashed through the dense, tangled underbrush in pursuit, grimacing in pain and clutching his injured parts guardedly when he failed to step with sufficient care. When he came upon the Indian tying the unconscious boy's hands and feet with rawhide strips, Bear stumbled to his knees, drawing the gleaming Bowie knife as he knelt over Billy's still form.

"I told the little shit what I'd do," he spat as he started to unbutton the boy's trousers.

The Sioux whacked Bear's wrist sharply with the handle of the heavy war club, and the knife went spinning into the brush. Bear clasped his throbbing wrist in agony and glared at the stone-faced Indian furiously.

His own black eyes meeting Bear's unflinchingly, the Sioux said firmly, "The boy is mine."

Bear's muscles tensed, and his face turned crimson. For a few moments there was an awkward, nervous silence during which a single threatening move or one misspoken word might have brought death to either of the antagonists.

Then Bear's outrage cooled slightly and he grumbled acrimoniously, "All right, Lone Badger, this little bastard sure as hell ain't worth fightin' over. You can have him. Now let's get the others." The big man rose slowly to his feet.

"No, we wait," said the Indian. "We are only five."

3

INSIDE THE SOD house Martha Kesterson lifted the cast-iron lid of the Dutch oven and pressed a golden biscuit lightly with her forefinger. The top of the biscuit sprang back and Martha nodded in approval.

Martha, in her early forties, was still a handsome woman. Her honey-colored hair was streaked only slightly with gray, and, although her waist was beginning to thicken, she was one of those women who held her age well. Martha hummed as she forked the hot biscuits from the black kettle-like oven and deposited them on a shiny tin platter. Her cheerful, pleasant face belied the trying tragic times she had endured since her family homesteaded in the Nebraska hills.

Five years earlier, a diphtheria epidemic had ravaged the county. When the rampaging disease hit the Kesterson homestead, Sam and Martha had nursed their three stricken children for endless hours without rest, tormented constantly by the coughing, choking delirium of their fevered sons and daughter. First Jane, two years Billy's senior, had succumbed and then Frank, and finally her second eldest, James, had died. Billy and Sarah had been unexplainably immune to any assault from the disease and, grateful that two of her children were spared, she had come to terms with her loss, accepting that she must carry on for the living.

Martha's daughter, Sarah, turned the thick, curling slices of bacon sizzling in the black, cast iron frying pan atop the burner of the cast-iron cooking stove. The aroma of coffee steamed from the huge pot next to the skillet. The big cook stove was Martha's single concession to luxury and occupied the prominent place in the cooking area of the room. Sam had had the stove shipped by railroad from the East as a gift for their twentieth wedding anniversary two years earlier. It was the newest model range and even had a small oven, but Martha still preferred her old Dutch oven resting on hot coals in the stone, open-hearth fireplace for baking.

"What's taking them so long?" Martha asked offhandedly.

Hot grease crackled and splattered from the frying pan and Sarah stepped back from the stove momentarily. "If I know Billy," she said, "he probably got Dad to help him check out his rabbit snares before they come in."

Sarah, a few months short of twenty, was a lithe, slender young woman with a fair, Nordic complexion, tanned only slightly by the simmering Nebraska sun. She was taller than the average woman of her time and her shimmering golden hair, pulled back and tied with a wide blue ribbon, reached to the small of her back. Full, ample, but not disproportionately large, breasts were evidenced by the womanly mounds that pressed against her flowered cotton dress. She had laughing mischievous eyes and a nose that was perhaps a bit too straight—the heritage of her Scandinavian ancestors. Her full lips covering white, even teeth seemed to be set in a perpetual, genial smile.

Sarah was an enigma even to her parents. Martha worried that Sarah's seeming contradictions scared off the many bachelor neighbors who might be prospective husbands. Her openness and wholesome good looks had drawn many a young farmer and rancher to the Kesterson homestead. After several visits, however, few called again. Martha had suggested to Sam that the young men were frightened by Sarah's keen intellect and defiant assertiveness. Sam had just laughed. "Not all men want a meek woman, Martha. God knows, you'd have never found a husband if they did. She'll meet her match one day."

Martha had not been appeased, however. She had a beautiful, eligible daughter who would soon be past prime marriageable age. On the one hand, Sarah was gentle and domestic with all of the feminine graces; on the other, she handled horses and a shotgun as well as or better than most men. At times, she lived in a dream world, writing poetry and little romantic stories; still, she thrived in the outdoors helping Sam round up the cattle or felling cottonwoods with an awesome, wicked, double-bladed axe. Sarah was warm and friendly; she could also be volatile and explosive.

Once, Sam had made what Martha thought was an unflattering comparison of Sarah to one of his old range cows. The scarred, grizzled cow was blind in one eye, the result of an infection incurred as a calf. Old One Eye, as Sam had called her, faithfully raised a big, hardy calf every year. She was the boss of the herd, the top of the pecking order. "Not even the bull messes with her till she's good and ready." Sam had observed. The other cows might come through the winter skin and bones, but old One Eye would always be fat and sassy. "She's the kind of cow that'll make this country," he had said. "That old devil's a survivor, and that's what Sarah is—a survivor."

Martha glanced out the narrow front window of the sod house, searching the path for Sam and Billy. The three-foot-thick walls of the soddy provided more insulation from the intense heat that was building up outside, but moist rings were already darkening the underarms of her rust-brown dress.

"Sarah, will you see what's keeping your father and Billy?" asked Martha as she turned to the stove. "If those two don't hurry up, they'll get a choice of cold or burned biscuits." She wrapped the skirt of her apron around the handle of the big, steaming coffee pot and placed it on the rough oak table.

Sarah pulled open the thick cottonwood door and started down the path to the creek. She stopped, spotting the two full water buckets resting on the creek bank at the foot of the hill. Her eyes scanned the creek banks uneasily.

"Dad!" she called. "Billy! Come on and eat." Glancing toward the barn, she caught sight of her father's fly-covered prostrate body. Automatically, she moved toward the still figure, when out of the corner of her eye she glimpsed movement of a shadow just inside the open barn door. She turned and dashed toward the house, choking back near-hysterical sobs as she ran. As she stumbled through the door, she pushed it shut and slammed the heavy wooden bar into its iron bracket. Back flat against the door, she faced her startled mother.

"Mother," she said frantically, "he's dead. Dad's dead. Out by the barn. There's somebody out there."

"Oh, my God!" Martha gasped. Stunned and distraught, she was silent for a moment. Then, "Billy. Where's Billy?"

"I don't know. I didn't see him."

"The guns," Martha said. "Get the guns." She moved to the north window of the sod house and, peering out cautiously, she could make out Sam's grotesque head and shoulders before her view was obstructed by the huge barn. The blood was drying now and was beginning to darken and brown. She turned her head away, her face a ghostly white, silent tears streaming down her cheeks.

Sarah darted quickly into the other room. Her father's double-barreled shotgun and old Henry rifle leaned against the wall in the corner near her parents' double bed. A worn, rawhide bag of shells was tied to the shotgun by a leather thong. She rummaged through the drawers of her father's oak chest and found a tin box containing his remaining Henry cartridges. Snapping up the guns and ammunition, she returned quickly to the main room.

She handed the shotgun and shell bag to Martha who positioned herself by the north window and readied the twin barrels. Sarah kept the weighty Henry and slipped to one of the two front windows, resting the barrel of the rifle on the sill. Sam had brought the Henry back from the war. A powerful gun, it could kill at one thousand yards and would fire sixteen times without reloading. According to Sam, Union soldiers had claimed that the Henry, loaded on Sunday, fired all week. Sarah knew how to use the weapon but not more than twenty cartridges remained in the tin box.

For nearly half an hour, the two women watched and waited. Intermittently, Martha shook spastically as her eyes came to rest on the gory head of her dead husband. The smothering heat was beginning to overtake the house and the back of Martha's dress was soaked with perspiration.

Suddenly, Sarah saw a huge, black-bearded man emerge from the foliage across the creek. He swaggered triumphantly through the shallow creek and stopped, hands on hips, on the creek bank near the abandoned water pails. "Mother," she whispered, "there's a man down by the creek. He's white."

"I'm sure I saw an Indian peek around the corner of the barn. This shotgun won't do much good at this range, though," said Martha.

Sarah said, "Just wait till he gets close."

The big, white man hollered, "Come on out, folks. We ain't gonna hurt nobody. Just want a few eats, that's all. Then we'll be on our way."

He was answered by the roar of the Henry, and he stumbled backward into the creek as he dodged the bullet whining past his ear.

Scrambling awkwardly from the cold creek, Bear sputtered, "That's just fine, friends. You want to play rough, we'll show ya a real good time." He scratched his groin, cackled and waved to the Indians. "Let's have a little fire, boys!" he yelled.

In a few moments, the small outbuildings were engulfed in flames. The horses were driven out of the barn and snagged quickly by the Sioux warriors. No sooner was the last horse out than heavy, black smoke curled skyward from the barn.

Shrill squeals of pigs and bawling of cattle broke the still morning as the Sioux commenced their ruthless, systematic slaughter of the livestock. A few cows penned in the barn had not been released by the Indians, and the putrid smell of burning flesh filled the air. The stench drifted through the windows of the sod house, and Sarah and Martha coughed and choked, fighting the tears that streamed involuntarily from their smoke-filled eyes.

Martha spied a painted, bare-chested Indian in front of the burning barn not far from Sam's body. The shotgun exploded futilely. She squeezed the trigger again and then stooped to reload. The shotgun blast drew the raiders' attention back to the house.

The back of the sod structure was windowless, so the Indians were forced to approach from the front or sides. Bear charged across the creek, bellowing orders as the warriors moved closer to the house. Sarah's Henry barked twice, kicking up dust near Bear's feet as he dived belly-flat against the dry, hard slope. The Indians weaved back and forth, crawling, leaping, and dodging so that Sarah could not get a clear shot. The rifle cracked twice again, but she could not maneuver the heavy weapon quickly enough to strike a moving target.

A torrent of bullets thudded against the sod walls as Sarah ducked below the sill. Martha rose to the window, sliding the big, double barrels of the shotgun searchingly along the ledge. A single shot pierced the quiet. Sarah turned, startled, when she heard the sharp clanging of metal against metal as the shotgun fell from its perch, bouncing against the cooking stove as it fell to the hard-packed earth floor. She shrieked as she saw her mother crumple and collapse next to the gun, a widening mass of scarlet saturating the bosom of her dress.

Leaning the Henry against the wall, she crawled quickly to Martha's side. "Mother! Mother!" she choked, grasping the woman's unfeeling hand. The gaping, gurgling hole at the base of Martha's throat and her pale, frozen face told Sarah that her cries were unheard. Shocked and dazed, she was jolted to her senses when she heard the scraping on the window frame as a

Sioux warrior started to crawl through the narrow opening. Sarah snatched up the shotgun as the Indian's hands grasped the ledge to pull himself through. She leveled the shotgun and watched tensely as his sinewy muscles tightened and an eerie, painted face and shoulders emerged through the window. She raised the shotgun calmly and squeezed the trigger. The explosion thundered and vibrated through the room; the Indian tumbled backward through the window, his nose and the right side of his face blown completely away, replaced by a red pulp of blood and bone fragments.

Wiping the splattered blood and stinging perspiration from her eyes, Sarah edged along the wall. She stopped when she heard the pounding and hammering that thundered against the bulky slabs that formed the door. Suddenly, the gleaming blade of Sam's own axe appeared through the splintered cottonwood. The bar snapped and the shattered door fell in. Another Sioux warrior, clad only in breechclout and buckskin leggings, leaped through the open doorway flourishing a blood-stained war axe menacingly. Upon seeing Sarah, he crouched, an evil grin parting his thin, wet lips as he advanced toward her with the war axe upraised. Again, she pulled the shotgun trigger, and the resulting blast hurled the warrior backward. His eyes bulged open in astonishment and puzzlement as the axe dropped from his hand, and, instinctively, he grasped at his belly in a hopeless attempt to catch the pulverized, bluish intestines that spilled from the massive hole there. He jerked convulsively and tumbled over Sarah's narrow bed that had rested so peacefully along the south wall of the soddy.

Sarah darted, shotgun in hand, for the rawhide shell sack on the floor near Martha's limp body. She reached in the sack frantically, pulling out two more shells, but before she could reload, the shotgun was twisted harshly from her hands and she was pushed to the floor by a heavy, booted foot. She squirmed to get away as a rifle butt slammed against her forehead, and she drifted into unconsciousness.

Minutes later, Sarah's eyelids twitched and blinked open. As she raised her head groggily from the floor, her eyes focused on Martha's stripped bloody skull. She swallowed hard and turned away. Struggling to her knees, she fingered the throbbing, tender bulge on her forehead and grimaced as she ran her fingers along the sensitive, moist gash enfolded within the swelling.

She was startled by the clanging and rattling of Martha's pans and looked up to see a tall, skinny, almost emaciated, Indian ransacking her mother's small cupboard. His long, matted hair was draped over filthy, wet, slippery looking shoulders, and slanted streaks of red and yellow adorned the warrior's brown cheeks giving him an evil, foreboding look. Another shorter, stockier warrior dragged the body of his dead companion through the open doorway. Sarah's eyes fixed upon the fresh, still bloody scalp of long, light brown hair that dangled from his rawhide waist band.

Suddenly, a rough, calloused hand yanked her head sideways and tilted her chin upward; her eyes met the dark, piercing eyes of Bear Jenkins. "Now ain't you a saucy, little morsel," he laughed. "Come on up and say howdy to ol' Bear." He jerked her up from her knees, squeezing her arm in a viselike grip until she bit her lips to keep from crying out. Bear chided, "Now, sweetheart, you just be nice to ol' Bear, and you might keep that pretty scalp of yours. Better yet, you might just get to come along and keep me company for a few days." The big man chuckled to himself and relaxed his grip momentarily.

Sarah tore loose and shot for the open door, but pulled up short when she confronted Lone Badger standing just outside. The Indian's expressionless, stoic face showed no emotion, but his hand tightened perceptibly on the bloodstained knife at his side. Sarah veered away from the opening and dashed to the far end of the room, backing against the wall, her wild eyes darting back and forth like a cornered animal. Lone Badger stood silently in the entryway while the other Sioux rummaged noisily in the small bedroom.

Bear closed in on Sarah, his broken, leering grin and a growing bulge in his trousers leaving no doubt about his intentions. "Come here, you yellow-haired bitch!" he croaked. "Papa Bear's gonna give you somethin' special."

He lunged for Sarah's arm, but she ducked swiftly away and he crashed against the wall. He charged after her and, this time, caught her wrist, twisting it viciously until she fell painfully to her knees. He slapped her sharply across the mouth. "Listen, Goldilocks. You do what I say or you're gonna be one dead little girl," he warned. Sarah tried to pull away and the big man slipped his Bowie knife from its sheath. Waving the wicked long-bladed knife in front of her eyes, he asked, "We gonna be friends or not?"

His jaw tightened, and his beady eyes said that she had better surrender—or die. She quit struggling. "Now, that's more like it, dolly," Bear chortled, loosening his grip on her arm. "Now you just stand still, and I'm gonna treat ya like a real lady."

His crusty, grimy hands shot out snatching the top of Sarah's dress, ripping, tearing, and pulling at her clothes until she stood stark naked in the room. Sarah remained silent and grim-faced.

Tears rolled down her cheeks, but angry defiance flashed in her eyes.

"My, my, my!" grinned Bear. "Ain't you got a nice pair of tits, honey. And just fetch your eyes on that," his eyes roamed down her firm, smooth belly to the dark triangle between her legs. "I'd wager you'd be just ripe for the pickin'.'"

Tossing his Bowie knife on the table, Bear unfastened his belt as he walked slowly toward Sarah. His buckskin breeches dropped to his knees, and his flushed, engorged organ sprang free. Sarah shivered involuntarily and edged away, but he grabbed her wrist and, in a single motion, flipped her to the hard dirt floor. Instantly, he was on top of her, pinning her arms to the floor, crushing the breath from her with his massive, corpulent paunch. She tried to turn her face from his foul, rotten breath as his open, panting mouth sought hers. Sarah winced and sobbed softly as he punched again and again, trying to gain entry. Finally, he penetrated brutally, and only then did she cry out, reacting to the searing pain of his savage thrusts. Bear huffed and wheezed as his body pounded against Sarah's with harsh, driving force. He grunted like a hog when release came, spittle dripping from the corners of his mouth. He withdrew abruptly and lifted his wet, slippery body away. As he stood and pulled up his greasy, dirty trousers, he kicked Sarah sharply in the ribs.

"Now, weren't that nice, sweetheart," he said, "and just think, you can always remember that ol' Bear gave it to you the first time." He laughed hysterically.

Lone Badger stepped silently through the entryway, and Bear turned to join the Indians in the looting of the house. Sarah crawled snaillike to the corner of the room and huddled there on the floor, her smoldering eyes following the big white man as he lumbered about the room.

The skinny Indian emerged from the bedroom, his arms loaded with plunder. He stopped short and stared impassively at the naked young woman curled up in the corner. He looked at Bear and queried him in guttural Sioux.

Bear fixed his eyes on Sarah and shook his head affirmatively. "You hear that, Goldilocks? Crazy Buffalo wants some, too. You'd be glad to oblige, wouldn't you?"

He turned to the Indian and said, "Give her a good humpin', Crazy Buffalo. We're gonna pull out with the boy. When you're done, kill her." He stooped and picked up Sam's Henry and, gathering up his spoils, stomped out of the house chuckling to himself. Lone Badger followed.

Sarah brightened appreciably upon hearing Bear's casual reference to Billy. Her eyes became alive and alert. Crazy Buffalo piled his bounty on the oak table, and, as he advanced deliberately toward her, Sarah heard the horses galloping away from the homestead. A deathlike hush fell upon the sod house, interrupted only by the unrelenting hum of the flies at work on the carnage left by the raiders.

The stone-faced Sioux was attired only in a filthy, buckskin breechclout and ankle-high moccasins. His protruding ribs seemed on the verge of breaking through the tight, wet skin of his chest. But Sarah's eyes were drawn to the bone-handled hunting knife suspended in a crude sheath from the rawhide thong that served as the Indian's belt. She remained crouched and unmoving in the corner. As the Indian neared, the pungent odor of sour horse manure and stale perspiration was overpowering. He stood above her, his dark eyes traveling up and down her body. He pulled his breechclout aside and was on her like a cat. She feigned submission and tumbled back down to the floor. As the Sioux pressed against her and reared his buttocks in anticipation of entry, Sarah's fingers closed around the smooth handle of the knife and slid it easily from the sheath. With a fierce, upward thrust, she plunged the keen-edged blade into the Indian's belly. His eyes popped out in shock, and his mouth flew open to scream, but his throat emitted only a gagging, choking sound as Sarah shoved him away, and he collapsed in a heap on the floor.

Knife in hand, Sarah rose and peered out the window. They were gone. Clothing was strewn throughout the house; she singled out some of her own and dressed. She pulled a quilt from her parents' bed and took a blanket from Billy's straw-filled mat beneath her own bed. Dry-eyed and grim, she covered her mother's rigid grotesque body with the blanket. Carrying the quilt, she stepped barefoot out of the sod house and proceeded purposefully to Sam's unmoving form. Flies rose in a black, buzzing swarm as Sarah draped the down-filled quilt over his body.

Until then, Sarah had been oblivious to the intense heat radiating from the barn as orange flames swallowed and consumed the large building. She backed away and turned her eyes upon the devastation and slaughter that surrounded her. She gazed blankly, like someone in a trance, at the mutilated carcasses of the cattle and hogs. Abruptly, she pivoted and ran back to the sod house. Shortly, she reemerged cradling the big shotgun that had been passed over by the invaders. She stepped quickly down the slope, through the creek, and into the dense undergrowth on the opposite side. There she crouched next to one of the towering cottonwoods and waited in fearful anticipation of the raiders' return.

4

SEVERAL MILES SOUTHEAST of the Kesterson ranch, Thomas Jefferson Carnes brushed the stinging sweat from his eyes and climbed the dry, grassy hillside toward the crude board shack perched at the summit. *Wasted the whole damn morning on that wheel*, he thought, glancing over his shoulder at the crippled wagon resting at the base of the hill near Rock Creek. As he neared the top of the incline, Tom caught the faint aroma of salt pork and beans, and could make out the painted homemade sign above the cabin door—Double C Cattle Co. Some cattle company—a half section of dying grass and fifty half-starved cows. It was a long way from Red Oaks plantation.

Tall, almost six feet two inches, and sandy haired, Tom had the bearing of an aristocrat. Hard and trim from the rugged ranch life, Tom still carried himself like the army officer he had been. A southerner by birth and temperament, Tom had been a boy during the Civil War, too young to serve in the Confederate Army, but he remembered with unflagging bitterness.

He was still haunted by the gory picture of his father impaled on the end of a Yankee bayonet while their elegant plantation home was being devoured by flames. The war had driven him from the beloved Virginia plantation and sent him, with Joseph, to the home of his father's kindly brother, Phillip Carnes. His lawyer uncle had seen to his material needs and had been instrumental in obtaining Tom's appointment to West Point two years after the war. When Phillip, as executor of John Carnes's will, had been forced to sell Red Oaks at a fraction of its worth, Tom had felt a deep sense of loss and loneliness. The void had never been filled, and sometimes Tom worried that his quest for roots was an unhealthy obsession.

Tom had excelled at the military academy, but he was a loner. The other cadets had looked to Tom for leadership, but not friendship. He knew that he was cool and detached, and that some invisible barrier kept him from true comradeship with the others. But far from being hurt, he had been gratified that his aloofness afforded him additional time during which to plan and dream.

Graduating with honors from the academy, he had been assigned as a green second lieutenant to Fort Laramie in Wyoming territory. He had reported for duty at Fort Laramie three years after the Treaty of 1868 which brought an uneasy peace with the Sioux. During his uneventful duty there, the fort was free from Indian assault, and Tom's own combat experience as a cavalry officer had been confined to a few skirmishes with Indian bands led by an obscure Oglala Sioux war chief called Crazy Horse. In his nearly four years at Fort Laramie, Tom advanced to the rank of captain. Only twenty-five years old, his progress was meteoric for the peacetime army. His military career was tagged by his superiors as promising.

But the preceding spring, Tom, to the shock and puzzlement

of the professional army, had resigned his commission and headed by train for Fairbury, Nebraska, the county seat of Jefferson County. He had been taken with the green, rolling hills of the county when he had passed through on his way to Fort Laramie. The sturdy oaks and enormous cottonwoods that lined the creek bottoms struck a responsive chord and rekindled his elusive dreams. Here he would build his own Red Oaks. . . . And he had never been comfortable wearing blue.

Tom paused in front of the shack and removed his sweat-soaked shirt. He liked the liberated feeling that the nakedness gave to his tight, muscular back and arms.

From his position on the crest of the hill, Tom could see for miles in every direction. He savored the view to the south where the rolling, grassy hills of Nebraska gave way to the more level acres of northern Kansas. Turning his eyes to the northwest, he observed thick, black smoke rising from behind a ridge and dissipating into expansive blue sky. It couldn't be a grass fire—the smoke was too localized and concentrated. Instinctively troubled and disquieted, he turned and paced more deliberately to the shack. As he entered the unkempt, single-room structure, he greeted the other half of Double C Cattle Company.

"Well, Joe, it doesn't smell too bad. Wouldn't matter anyhow. I'm hungry enough right now to eat fried buffalo chips if I had to."

"You just might have to," the other countered, "if you aren't a little more complimentary of the cook."

Joe turned toward Tom, skillet in hand, and grinned broadly. He was easily several inches taller than Tom and had wide, massive shoulders. The sinewy muscles that spanned his arms and chest stretched his denim shirt to its limits. The smooth, mahogany-hued skin of his face was embellished with a dashing, black mustache that draped just slightly over his lips. Joe was a handsome man by any standard, and his easy smile had, no doubt, dissolved the defenses of many a young woman.

Many former slaves had adopted the last names of their masters, but Joseph Carnes also carried his master's seed. It had been common knowledge on Red Oaks plantation that Joe was also John Carnes's son. Tom's mother had died giving birth to her son. Soon after, it was household gossip that Becky, a captivating, ebony servant girl, was sharing her master's bed. A bit more than a year after Tom's birth, Sally bore a son.

In the years that followed, Sally became mistress of the house in all but name. She occupied her own room on the master's floor and administered the day-to-day operation of the household. Joe shared Tom's private tutor and was permitted only occasionally to play with other Negro children on the plantation. Like most other southern plantation owners of his era, John Carnes rationalized and supported the institution of slavery, but he was also a kind man and gentle with the slave population of the plantation. He refused, often at considerable financial sacrifice, to break up Negro families and even maintained a small school for the slave children. Red Oaks slaves were frequently labeled "uppity" by the Carneses' neighbors.

When Joseph was ten years old, he and his mother had been formally granted their freedom by John Carnes, and, although the prized documents were no longer required, Joseph still carried them with his valuables as proof that he was a free man before Abe Lincoln came along. Nonetheless, Joe and Sally had remained at Red Oaks as free blacks and an informal part of the Carnes family. Sally died shortly after the start of the war, but it was accepted as a matter of course that Joe would continue residing in the home with unacknowledged status of son and brother.

After John Carnes's death, Joe was taken into the Phillip Carnes home with Tom for a brief spell. He was promptly assigned servant duties and, although he and Tom had remained close, he was unable to accept the new family relationship. One morning, he decided to leave and head west.

The railroad had offered a natural home for Joe's talents. Although not more than a boy, with his enormous size and strength, he quickly landed a job with a Negro crew, laying rails for the Union Pacific near Omaha. His innate intelligence and obvious education made him a natural link between management and the unskilled, uneducated Negro workers. In a short time, he had been made foreman of his own crew.

Later, he was assigned as liaison to a band of Pawnee scouts employed by the Union Pacific to protect its crews from Sioux and Cheyenne attacks as the railroad wormed its way across the Nebraska plains. He became fast friends with many of the Pawnee warriors who were in awe of the black man's towering physique and overpowering strength. He was called Black Bull by the Pawnee in honor of the bull buffalo that was so highly worshipped and respected by the Plains Indians. Joe found ready acceptance among the Pawnee and had even taken a Pawnee wife who had been tragically killed in a Sioux raid on their village during one of Joe's long absences. In his years with the Pawnee, Joe honed and sharpened his skills as a frontiersman, and by May of 1869, when the tracks of the Union Pacific were joined with the Central Pacific at Promontory Point in Utah, Black Bull had become something of a legend.

In the years that followed, Joe continued working for the Union Pacific, mostly as a scout and troubleshooter for construction and maintenance crews. Between assignments, he lived with the Pawnee. He and Tom exchanged letters when they could, and, after Tom's assignment to Fort Laramie, they were able to meet once or twice a year. At their last meeting before Tom's resignation from the army, Tom had related his plans. Uncle Phillip was holding Tom's small inheritance from his father, and Tom had accumulated some money of his own, and Tom proposed they pool their capital and have a try at ranching. Joe, ready to try something new, agreed. He was to ride to Fairbury and scout out the possibilities; Tom would join him as soon as he was discharged.

Tom eased into a chair at the rustic, cottonwood-hewn table as Joe scraped chunks of salt pork, smothered with steaming beans, from a greasy, black skillet into two tin plates. Setting the plates at the table and taking his own seat, Joe asked casually, "Did you see that smoke off to the northwest this morning?"

"I just saw it when I came up. How long has it been going?" Tom replied.

Joe said, "I noticed it when I was working out by the horse barn about midmorning—it hasn't died down much since then. It's all shooting up from one place. It's not likely a grass fire. Could be trouble for somebody."

Tom queried, "Who lives over that way, do you know?"

"A family name of Kesterson, I think. Small ranchers."

The Virginians had lived in the county for less than half a year, having purchased the tiny ranch and small herd of stock cows with the last of their funds. Their only real acquaintances in the county were the lawyer in Fairbury who had helped with the land acquisition, and the storekeeper at nearby Steele City where they purchased most of their supplies. So far, they had kept pretty much to themselves—Tom, because of his natural penchant for isolation; Joe, although, more extroverted, because years of living with his race had taught him to proceed cautiously.

The men ate ravenously and quietly until Tom broke the silence. "You feel like a ride this afternoon?"

Joe answered, "I thought you were just going to move out here, build a big ranch house and mind your own business. I don't know why the Sioux didn't lift your scalp out in Fort Laramie country, anyway. If you'd had your eyes open, you'd have seen that there are two horses tied down by the barn—saddled and ready to go." Joe grinned, as he rose from the table. "Let's hit the road, partner. You can do the dishes when we get back."

5

THEY SMELLED IT before they saw it. The two riders, the lighter man mounted on a sleek bay mare and the larger man astride a big-boned spirited, white gelding, made their way warily along the red clay banks of Rock Creek. They stopped intermittently to listen, catching only the steady hum of the creek waters and the labored breathing of their own sweating horses.

It was mid-afternoon when they led their horses into the clearing. The stench was almost unbearable and Tom struggled to retain his dinner. During his duty in Wyoming, he had viewed some of the butchery and mutilation inflicted by the Oglala Sioux; there was no doubt in his mind about who had visited the Kesterson homestead. As he surveyed the smoldering debris and bloating carnage, he felt indignation and outrage at the waste and senselessness of it all.

He lifted his wide-brimmed hat, sighed, and brushed back his damp, coarse sandy hair. A dark shadow swooped across his forehead. Shielding his green-brown eyes from the blinding sun momentarily, he looked upward and caught sight of the black, sinister-looking turkey vultures that had been interrupted in their work and soared above the smoldering outbuildings, their wide, outspread wings casting floating shadows on the ground.

"Jesus Christ," choked Joe. "They've been slaughtered. Every Goddamn last living thing's been slaughtered!"

They tied their horses at the edge of the clearing. Tom slipped his Winchester carbine easily from the rawhide loop that suspended the rifle from the saddle. He had opted for the cavalry technique of carrying the weapon on horseback in lieu of the bulkier, more cumbersome, saddle holster used by most cattlemen. The twelve-shot repeating saddle gun was the companion piece to the Colt "Peacemaker" revolver resting in the holster on his right hip. Both guns conveniently accepted the .44 centerfire cartridges and were welcome improvements to the antiquated, outmoded army firearms.

The two men walked slowly and cautiously into the open yard—Joe's fingers brushing the cold steel of his own six-shooter, Tom cradling the Winchester in readiness. They stepped up to the quilt-covered corpse of Sam Kesterson near the smoking timbers of the barn. Joe bent over and pulled back the bloody cover. "Must be Kesterson," he observed matter-of-factly as his eyes fell upon Sam's crushed, disfigured head. Releasing the quilt, he scanned the fringes of the clearing searchingly. "Somebody lived to tell about it or he wouldn't have been covered up."

Not far from the sod house, they found the gruesome bodies of two Sioux, a trail of dried, brown blood leading from the open doorway indicating that one of the victims had been dragged from the house. "Somebody sure as hell used a shotgun on those two," Tom pointed out. Then, tugging at the rawhide medicine pouch that adorned the neck of one of the dead Indians, "They're Sioux, all right."

The Oglala, one of the tribes of the Teton Sioux, believed that all the powers they needed were controlled by various gods. When a Sioux boy approached manhood, he went alone into the wilderness where he fasted, prayed, tortured himself, and waited for a vision. Upon returning to the village, he went to the medicine man who interpreted his vision and identified the boy's guardian spirit. The spirit might dwell in any object—a bird, an animal, even a plant. The Oglala boy would then obtain some part of the guardian spirit, perhaps a feather or a bone, and carry it with him at all times, frequently in a small rawhide pouch. This was his reservoir of personal power.

Tom led the way through the open doorway. In a few moments, both men emerged choking and coughing from the heavy, putrefying odor that permeated the house. They had stayed just long enough to note that the dead occupants were a Sioux warrior and a middle-aged white woman, and then they promptly evacuated the premises.

Tom said, "I'm afraid we've got some nasty work to do. Tell you what, Joe, we'll draw straws to see who takes the house."

"Go to hell," Joe answered, and walked away to the barn. Kicking away burnt, smoking debris, Joe scrounged through the rubble, retrieving any salvageable tools and implements. Picking up a rusty spade attached to a charred stub, he froze when he caught movement in the brush across the creek. Slowly, he moved toward Tom who was backing clumsily out of the soddy, his hands locked on the ankles of the dead Sioux.

"Tom," Joe whispered, "don't turn around, but somebody's in the bushes across the creek. On three, hit the dirt. One . . . two . . . three."

The stiff, rigid legs of the dead Indian thumped against the earth and both men, drawing their Colts, dived to the ground pointing their pistols in the direction of the cottonwood grove.

Abruptly, the brush beneath he trees parted and Sarah waded into the creek. The two men rose as she walked calmly and soberly up the worn path, her hands gripped tightly on the shotgun. Holstering his Peacemaker, Tom hesitated and then stepped quickly to meet the young woman.

She was a pathetic sight—wet, tangled hair, her sweaty grimy face speckled with blood, and a bluish purple lump covering half of her forehead. As she drew closer, Tom could make out attractive feminine features that suggested a dormant beauty slept beneath the dirty, weary face. But he was stricken especially by the young woman's eyes, ice-blue, intelligent eyes, but cold and unfeeling. There were no tears, no outward signs of the intense sorrow she must feel.

He moved to relieve Sarah of the heavy shotgun. He had expected the disheveled, exhausted young woman to collapse sobbing in his arms. Instead, Tom knew she had eyed him appraisingly before surrendering the shotgun, and now her mind was obviously turning to the immediate tasks at hand.

Ill at ease, he introduced himself, "Ma'am, my name's Tom Carnes," and gesturing toward the Negro, "and this is my brother, Joe Carnes. We live south of here a few miles and saw the smoke from your ranch." Then softly, he murmured, "I'm sorry. This must have been your family."

She responded dispassionately, "Yes, my mother's in the cabin, and that's my father." She nodded her head in the direction of Sam's prone body. "We were attacked by Indians led by a white man. One Indian and a white man—he called himself Bear—took my brother Billy. When I heard your horses, I thought they were returning. I have to get my brother back, but first there's work to be done here. I'd be grateful for your help."

Tom had the uneasy feeling that her polite quest was nearer a command than a plea for help. Tom was accustomed to giving orders and was mildly perplexed at the turnabout. He looked questioningly at Joe. The latter's face was expressionless, but there was an annoying twinkle in his dark eyes.

"Well, Captain Carnes," he said, "I'll see if I can fix that shovel."

6

THANK GOD, THAT'S done, Tom thought as he stood solemnly by Sarah near the two fresh mounds of black dirt. They had dug a shallow common grave for the three Indians and had buried Sam and Martha near the graves of their three children. Joe had fashioned a crude wooden cross and erected it midway between the graves of Sam and Martha. The tediously carved inscription read simply, "Sam and Martha Kesterson—August 16, 1875."

As they walked silently away from the graves, Tom breathed a sigh of relief. It had been an unpleasant, miserable job and he was damn glad it was over. There was nothing more they could do about the bloating carrion that was scattered about the homestead. They would have to leave that to the coyotes and turkey vultures and other carnivorous predators to clean up the mess.

He couldn't understand what kept Sarah going. She had been dry-eyed and almost serenely calm during the entire macabre process. She had unflinchingly undertaken to dress her parents for burial and, having accomplished that, had spent the remainder of the afternoon straightening up the house and packing the few items of personal belongings that had been overlooked by the raiders.

It was drawing close to sundown. What were they going to do with this young woman? She sure as hell couldn't stay here alone and, as far as Tom knew, he and Joe might be the closest neighbors. They could take her to Fairbury or Steele City, but, riding double, it would be well after dark when they got there. Tom and Sarah paused in front of the sod house, and Joe strolled on toward the horses.

As if reading Tom's mind, Sarah tilted her head upward, meeting Tom's eyes directly. "Mr. Carnes," she said, "do you suppose I might impose upon your hospitality a bit further and stay at your ranch tonight? I won't stay long; I plan to go after Billy in the morning."

Taken aback, he answered, "Uh, certainly, Miss Kesterson. I was just going to ask you if you'd like to stay. I have to warn you that our accommodations aren't exactly luxurious, though."

She knew he wouldn't say no. She was reading him like a book; you could see that in her eyes. Those damned eyes, he thought.

Joe saddled the horses, and they were ready to move out. Joe had remained strangely, and, uncharacteristically, quiet most of the afternoon, but somehow Tom had the feeling that the black man found a subtle humor in some part of the tragic situation— something to do with Tom's ineptness in dealing with the young woman.

Sarah went into the house, and when she returned, Tom was pleasantly surprised at the small bundle of personal belongings she carried. He'd expected he would have to weed out some of her possessions, but she apparently had the good sense to know there was a limit to the load the horses could carry.

Tom moved to assist her with her belongings. "Let me help you, Miss Kesterson," he said.

"Thank you," she responded and then, for the first time, with just the faintest trace of a smile, "but make it Sarah from now on."

"Okay, Sarah; I'm Tom. I'm afraid there are only two horses," Tom explained the obvious. "We'll have to ride double."

"That's fine," said Sarah. "Joe's horse is bigger; I'll ride behind him."

Joe mounted the white gelding. He added no comment, but his wide grin said it all. Then he asked with mock politeness, "Captain, would you like to help the young lady on the horse?"

Tom reddened noticeably and moved to help Sarah, but she'd already grabbed Joe's brawny arm, and he was pulling her onto the horse behind him.

Ill-humoredly, Tom mumbled, "Let's head for home."

7

TOM WRIGGLED HIS way out of the tangled blankets heaped in front of the Double C Cattle Company shack. He stretched and rubbed the sore spots on his thighs and shoulders, souvenirs from the night on the rocky ground.

A quail whistled his friendly "bobwhite" from the brush-filled ravine east of the barn. A meadowlark's throaty warble joined in to form a wilderness duet. A Nebraska sunrise was tough to beat. It was Tom's favorite time of day, and he almost never failed to be enraptured by the early morning bird chorus.

As he rose from his twisted bedroll, a soft breeze stirred the air around the cabin discernibly to provide the tranquil hilltop with brief, welcome respite from the heat. It was inconceivable to Tom as he beheld the entrancing, undulating waves of prairie grass that this same serene land could beget the savagery and violence that had fallen upon the Kesterson ranch just one sunrise before.

A few paces away, Joe was lost in deep, untroubled sleep, his head propped at an uncomfortable angle against his worn, Texas-style saddle. He breathed evenly, but heavily, spicing the steady tempo only occasionally with a quick, comical snort.

It had been nearly dark when they returned from the Kesterson homestead. They had eaten sparingly of some crusty bread and dried beef jerky, washing it down with potent, hot coffee. After supper, Sarah had collapsed, exhausted, on Tom's wobbly cot and was quickly overtaken by sleep. The two men, in unspoken agreement, had put together their bedrolls and moved outside.

This morning, Tom was ravenous and his stomach growled hungrily in confirmation. Damn, it was his day to cook, so he had better get at it.

The cabin door creaked open and Sarah stuck her head out. "Tom, do you suppose you could see about some water? And it looks like you have a little smokehouse out back. If there's a ham hanging in there, I'll see if I can scratch up some breakfast."

"Sure enough." His earlier enthusiasm bounced back, and he set out on the errands.

Upon returning with a large, smoked ham, Sarah thanked him properly, but somewhat indifferently, and suggested that he tend to his chores outside. As he walked to the barn, he had an uneasy feeling that the young woman had assumed command again.

Later, as Tom grained the horses, Joe sauntered into the barn. "Morning, Captain. Things look a little brighter today?" he chuckled.

Until the events of the last twenty-four hours, Joe had never called him Captain, and this was becoming a point of some irritation. "What in the hell's with this 'Captain' business?" he queried.

Joe answered mischievously, "Well, I just thought you were

entitled to a little respect. And I sure don't think you're going to get it from the little lady in the house."

Tom's eyes sparked testily, but he said nothing.

The aroma of fresh biscuits and frying ham drew Tom and Joe back to the cabin. When he stepped into the single room, Tom blinked in wonderment at the transformation that had taken place in a few short hours. Dirty pans and plates had been washed, the floor swept, and even the table scrubbed clean.

But the biggest change of all was Sarah. She still inhabited the dusty, torn dress she had worn the day before, and raw, inflamed scratch marks decorated her fair cheeks and neck. The ugly lump on her forehead had diminished, leaving a huge blue-black bruise that contrasted sharply with her golden tresses as it extended into her hairline. But now, her soft, shiny hair was brushed out and combed back and tied with a piece of red cloth. Now her skin had a clean, healthy glow, and it seemed to Tom that Sarah's eyes had softened visibly. At this moment, he was very much aware there was a woman in the room.

Sarah joined the men at the table, and they ate hungrily, devouring the thick slices of ham and hot biscuits quickly. "This is mighty good, Sarah," Joe said. "We don't eat this good very often, especially when my partner here cooks."

Ignoring Joe's good-humored dig, Tom agreed, "When I was in the army, only generals ate this well, Sarah."

"Thank you," she responded. "You're both very kind." A trace of a smile formed on her lips.

Savoring another cup of steaming coffee as they sat leisurely at the table, Joe and Tom made small talk, carefully avoiding any reference to the events of the previous day. Sarah had seemed distant and preoccupied throughout breakfast, and Tom was reluctant to broach the subject of her future.

Abruptly, Sarah announced matter-of-factly, "I'll be leaving to go after Billy this afternoon. I could use some help rounding up horses and supplies."

The men exchanged startled glances. Joe shrugged and poured another cup of coffee. Tom protested, "Sarah, we can't just let you run off after your brother like that. I'm sorry—I don't want to be callous—but we don't even know if your brother's alive. And if he is, the renegades are already miles ahead. One of us will ride into Fairbury and tell the county sheriff what's happened. He'll get word to the army and other authorities. That's your only hope. The best thing we can do is to help you get situated with some friends or family and—"

Sarah interrupted, indignation flashing in her eyes. "Listen, Mr. Carnes. Don't talk to me in that damned patronizing tone. I know what kind of country this is. In the last twenty-four hours, my parents have been murdered, I've been raped, and my brother's been dragged off to God-knows-where. Friends or family? Billy is my family, and I'm going to find him and bring him home where he belongs."

Tom was stunned momentarily. This young woman, who had been so domestic and feminine a few moments before, had unashamedly confirmed the worst of his suspicions and defiantly proclaimed her independence.

Joe cast his eyes downward and toyed casually with his coffee cup. Tom's annoyance increased when he caught the outline of a smile on Joe's lips. His face flushed, and he stood to leave the table.

"Well, dammit, you'll do it without any help from us. If there's one thing I learned in the army—"

"Mr. Carnes," she said icily, "I don't give a damn what you learned in the army. . . . And I haven't seen any signs so far that it could have been very much." She paused and untied her apron, tossing it to Tom who snagged it reflexively. "I hope you learned to do dishes in the army," she said.

Their eyes locked, each meeting the other's angry glare; each refusing to back off and walk away.

Joe broke the impasse, speaking softly. "Sarah, I've got a feeling you already have a list of the provisions you'll need. If you'll give it to me, I'll get over to the general store in Steele City and pick up supplies. I have a tough old black gelding I'll lend you for the trip."

Sarah, scorning Tom willfully, moved gracefully to her bundle of personal belongings already assembled on Tom's cot. She whisked out a ragged piece of brown paper and handed it to Joe. "The trousers and shirts on the list are for me, Joe. You'll just have to do the best you can for size. The boots I brought from home should be okay, but I could use a hat. We have a good herd of range cows with calves at side—the Indians didn't get them. Do you suppose you could make a deal with the storekeeper to sell twenty of the cows and calves? I'll take half in cash, and he can deduct the supplies from the balance and hold what's left till I get back. He'll have to find somebody to cut out his share of the cows. . . . Maybe he could even get somebody to ride over and check things out every few days."

Miffed at his obvious exclusion from the proceedings, Tom sat back down at the table and glowered coldly at Sarah. Her eyes met his again briefly, but they were dismissive and expressionless. It was just as if he weren't in the room. Damn, stubborn woman.

Joe said, "There's an old Pawnee who hangs around the livery stable in Steele City most of the time. We're going to need a top-notch tracker real bad, Sarah, and I've ridden with the old bird before. He'd be mighty handy to have around in a pinch. I'll see what it takes to get him to go with us. Not much, I'll bet."

Surprised and riled again, Tom interjected, "What do you mean 'we'?"

Joe countered, "Well, I thought maybe I'd just take a little vacation." Then turning to Sarah he added, "That is if the lady doesn't mind."

"The lady would be most grateful," Sarah said with noticeable relief.

Joe looked resolutely at Tom. "I'll be riding out with her. I'd take it real kindly if you'd look after the place while we're on the trail. Any orders, Captain."

Sighing and shaking his head in surrender, Tom said, "Yeah. Make arrangements for someone to look after our damn cows, too. . . . And add supplies for another man." He got up and stomped out the door.

8

JOE RODE IN from Steele City shortly after midday leading two sturdy pack horses loaded with supplies. He was followed by a squat, gnome-like man astride a sleepy eyed paint.

Stone Dog, who had been nicknamed Stony by farmers and ranchers in the Steele City area, was a walnut-brown Pawnee. His disproportionately large head was set on a stubby, pot-bellied body, and long, straggly, black hair splashed with white dropped over his narrow shoulders. The thick, red eyelid of his left eye opened to reveal a scarred, corrugated eyeball completely devoid of its iris. This, coupled with his wrinkled, prune-like face, gave the Indian a strangely grotesque appearance. He wore denim trousers, faded to a pale blue, and, in spite of the heat, a heavy, plaid flannel shirt. Deerskin moccasins covered his feet and a single feather was set in the battered, dusty black hat that concealed most of his forehead.

Joe announced, "Sarah . . . Tom . . . this is Stone Dog. We scouted together for the U.P. When I told him we were going after some Sioux, he jumped at the chance to come along."

Tom, who was sullenly filling his saddle bags, paused and

nodded his greeting. The old devil must be a hundred. Well, they already had to drag along a sharp-tongued female, a doddering, old Indian ought to just about round out the ticket.

Sarah rushed eagerly over to the old Indian, extending her hand. Startled at her openness, the Pawnee almost tumbled off the paint. He accepted her hand, and as she squeezed his warmly, the corners of his mouth moved upward and a few drops of chewing tobacco slipped down his chin. Tilting her head upward to meet the Indian's steady gaze, Sarah smiled gratefully. "I can't tell you how happy I am you're coming with us."

Tom saw the Indian nod in obvious satisfaction. Well, she had won the Indian over. He was sure as hell going to be outvoted on this trip. It would be a hell of a note if women ran for public office. Damned if she would get his vote, though.

Dismounting, Joe reported, "I've got your things, Sarah," and ambling over to one of the pack horses, he removed several bulky, paper-wrapped bundles. Sarah took the packages from Joe and nodded approvingly.

"I'll be ready in half an hour," she said and withdrew into the shack.

While they waited for Sarah, Joe and Tom finished saddling and packing the horses. The old Indian waited stoically on his spotted pony.

Joe assured Tom that the venerable Pawnee wasn't as old as he looked—and a hell of a lot smarter. Moreover, Sarah and the Indian shared a common tragedy. Stone Dog's wife and only son had been murdered by the Sioux, and a Sioux warrior was somehow responsible for his sightless eye. The Indian's hatred for the Sioux made him an eager ally, and his native instincts and intelligence would make him invaluable on the trail, Joe insisted.

Tom glanced doubtfully again at the silent Indian.

Joe also had learned that the man called Bear was more than likely Elijah Jenkins, an adopted member of an Oglala Sioux band. He lived with a Sioux woman and raided with a band of scavengers who barely had respectability in the eyes of their own people. They terrorized isolated areas throughout northern Kansas, Nebraska, and South Dakota, always returning in the fall to the tribe's main camp in the Black Hills of South Dakota. Jenkins was said to be a crude, brutal, unfeeling man. Tom thought the latter observation was unnecessary.

Horses saddled and packed, Tom thrust his carbine in its saddle loop. Then, almost tenderly, he picked up a long, gleaming saber and wrapped its wicked blade with rawhide, leaving only the shiny, gold-colored hilt exposed, and lashed the weapon to the bedroll behind his saddle. He was pretty handy with the cavalry officer's saber, and it had seen him through a few rough scrapes during his duty at Fort Laramie. Tom was just superstitious enough that he wasn't going to embark on this wild goose chase without it, as out of place as it might seem.

Shortly, Sarah emerged from the shack, shotgun cradled in her arms, and the Sioux hunting knife suspended in a stiff, new sheath on her belt. Beneath her yellow straw hat, you could see that her golden hair had been sheared below her neck and ears. The tight-fitting denim pants and shirt could not deny her ample feminine figure, however, and Tom averted his eyes from her quizzical look as he realized he had been staring at her. Damn, why did this woman make him feel so incompetent and childish?

"Sarah, you are some beautiful lady." Joe grinned.

Blushing, Sarah's eyes softened, and her tough shell cracked for just a moment. She smiled warmly, "Thank you, Mr. Carnes, you've made my day," and curtsied teasingly.

Just as quickly, the businesslike Sarah returned. "Before we go, I think we should all have an understanding. Somebody's got to be in charge—give the orders, have the final say-so." Her eyes jumped from one man to the other.

Tom mumbled sarcastically to himself, "Oh, hell! Now she's got to have a title, too." He leaned against his horse and squeezed the saddle-horn until his knuckles turned white, kicking impatiently at the dirt.

Sarah looked directly at Tom. "I think it's only logical that Tom be the leader. He was an officer at Fort Laramie and Joe says he was a darned good one."

Tom straightened, and, taken by surprise, reddened slightly. Stone Dog grunted his approval; Joe, mockingly, came to attention.

"What are your orders, Captain?"

Sarah moved closer and offered her hand. Hesitating momentarily, Tom took it, and for the first time, saw genuine warmth in her eyes. "Truce?" she asked.

"Truce," he replied. He released her hand reluctantly. "Okay, saddle up."

9

As THEY RODE away from the Double C Ranch, Tom looked over his strange patrol. It was an unlikely, incongruous band that circumstances had brought together. Of course, he'd let Joe cover his back any time. What about the Pawnee? Well, he still had to be convinced. Sarah was a mystery. She was so utterly different from any woman he'd ever encountered, and he felt almost overwhelmed by the ambivalence of his emotions about her. She was a disturbing force to say the least.

As they drew farther away from the ranch, Tom queried the Indian, "Stone Dog, you're the scout. Where do we start?"

"Kesterson ranch," he answered.

An hour later, the four riders entered the clearing. The charred remains of the barn were still smoldering and the air reeked of death and decay. It was the hottest time of day, and the atmosphere was suffocating.

"Well, it hasn't gotten any prettier," Joe said.

Stone Dog slipped from his horse with an agility that belied his physique. Bounding from place to place, eyes and nose almost touching the ground at times, he reminded Tom of a nervous

Virginia foxhound trying to pick up a scent.

While they waited for the Indian to finish his probing search of the premises, Tom and Joe watered the horses. Sarah, her face masked and emotionless, followed Stone Dog about the homestead, deliberately maintaining her silence. She eyed the Pawnee curiously when he would stop from time to time and kneel to sift through some apparently significant sign.

As Sarah and the Pawnee headed back to the horses, Sarah revealed the first crack in her confident demeanor. "Stone Dog," she implored softly, "I want to know the truth. What are the chances that Billy's still alive?"

"If brother's smart like golden lady, he lives," Stone Dog answered impassively, in his rasping, gravel voice. It was the longest statement any of his companions had heard the wizened, brown man utter. He climbed on his paint and grunted, "This way." He reined the pony northwest, and as his horse trotted away from the clearing, the others fell in behind.

They rode until nearly sunset, stopping only intermittently for water or for Stone Dog to scrutinize the trail. They left the rolling, grassy hills of southern Jefferson County behind and traveled into the dense, thickly wooded bottomlands of the Little Blue River. They followed the clear, sandy-bottomed river upstream along its winding, westerly course. Soon, Stone Dog dismounted again, scouring the damp river bank where other tracks had obviously joined those of the pursued.

"Now they are ten," he said.

Joe observed, "They must have split off into several raiding parties and now they're getting back together. That's not good."

Tom said, "I think we've gone far enough for tonight. It'll be dark soon. We'll camp here."

Sarah opened her mouth to protest and then, catching herself, in reluctant agreement, slid off her horse.

They made their camp beneath the green ash and gigantic cottonwoods that flourished in the moist, black silt along the bottomlands. Wood was plentiful, and Joe and Sarah built a small cooking fire while Tom tended to the horses. Stone Dog had left the camp but came back shortly with two plump jack rabbits. Later, a hush fell over the camp as the orange, glowing fire crackled hypnotically, and they silently devoured roasted rabbit and left-over biscuits.

Tom studied Sarah's face furtively. It seemed detached, almost imperturbable, but her clear, blue eyes betrayed a deep melancholy and depression. Inexplicably, he was deeply disturbed and troubled by the young woman's sadness and was frustrated by his inability to cope with it. He was driven by an urge to gather her into his arms and hold her and comfort her tenderly.

Finally, terminating the uneasy silence, Tom rose and moved to wash his tin plate in the boiling kettle of water at the fire's edge. "Better hit the sack pretty soon," he murmured.

Tom and Joe stretched out their bedrolls side by side not far from the fire. Tom felt his small party should sleep in reasonably close proximity in case of surprise attack, but he was reluctant to mention it to Sarah. Again, his concerns were unfounded as Sarah approached his sleeping place and, without comment, rolled out her blankets next to his. With a quick, distrustful glance at Tom, Stone Dog positioned himself on the other side of Sarah. Sarah pulled off her boots and slipped swiftly into the blankets, falling instantly into a deep, exhausted slumber.

Tom unfastened his gun belt and placed it within easy reach, not far from his head. Tugging at his damp boots, he glanced to his right and winced at the sight of Joe grinning mockingly at him in the dark. The mulatto winked knowingly and rolled over.

Looking uneasily to his left, his eyes paused on the peaceful, now almost childlike, face of the young woman turned to him in her sleep. As he stretched out in his blankets, Sarah stirred momentarily and edged closer to him. He could not escape the erotic images that danced in his brain when he felt her soft body pressing innocently against him through the blankets. Then his southern conscience chastised him harshly. Was he really any better than the man who had raped this young woman?

Tom was not a man of vast sexual experience, but he had romped with a few whores in his time and was secure in his manhood. He had even pierced the virginity of a snobbish, but very horny, young woman during an intimate interlude in Cheyenne while he was on a brief furlough from Fort Laramie. He had gone on from his earlier escapades with no feelings of remorse or guilt.

Why was he caught up in this cross fire of emotions when it came to Sarah? Sometimes, she seemed so alone and vulnerable, he wanted to hold and protect her; at other times she appeared so strong and competent, he was compelled to fight and establish his own dominance. There were times he just wanted to be alone with Sarah, to talk and share. But now, he just wanted her. Damn, he thought, I'm losing my mind. Eventually, he escaped into an uneasy and tormented sleep.

10

ALMOST FORTY MILES upriver, embers of another fire glowed in the dark, still night. The blond fair-skinned boy huddled at the base of a gnarled oak was a sharp contrast to the brown, black-haired men hunkered around the fire.

Billy Kesterson's round, blue eyes darted uncertainly from face to face. He was frightened. After Bear and Lone Badger had been joined by another band, the raiders had embarked on an orgy of slaughter, burning, and looting. He had caught a glimpse of his father's gory body, and the matted scalp hanging from Lone Badger's belt was a continual reminder of his mother's fate. Bear had bragged that one of the warriors had remained behind to deal with Sarah, but he had overheard Bear grumbling and fretting because the Indian had not shown up yet.

He had learned quickly not to resist. The reddish-purple mass covering the right side of his face attested to what he could expect if he refused to cooperate.

Billy gazed somberly at the fire, listening to, but not comprehending, the alien gibberish of his Oglala captors. Bear and Long Badger spoke alternately in English and Sioux dialect, often shifting from one language to the other in the middle of a conversation.

Billy had ridden exhaustedly with the Sioux as they blazed their bloody trail along the Little Blue valley. He had seen other children murdered ruthlessly, but no other captives were taken. Bear roughed him up at every opportunity but made no further attempts on his life.

Lone Badger was the leader of the little band and made it clear to the others that Billy was under his protection. The stocky Oglala had lashed Billy's bare back viciously on several occasions since his capture and struck Billy's face repeatedly when he had struggled to escape. Once Billy ceased his resistance, however, the Sioux became more subdued, almost motherly, on occasion. He made an onion-smelling plaster and administered it gently to the inflamed welts that peppered Billy's back and, although Billy's wrists were still bound in front of him, the Indian had untied his ankles so he could move about more freely. Billy brightened with the improved treatment, but fear had crept into his eyes earlier that evening when Lone Badger, grinning devilishly, had stooped down and run his hand up and down the inside of Billy's thigh, pinching at his rump much like his father used to do when he was picking a fat hog to butcher.

Billy's attention was drawn away from the flickering fire when he observed Lone Badger and another warrior mounting their ponies and riding silently out of the camp. Turning back to the fire, his eyes met Bear glaring scornfully at him across the small flame. The big man's lips parted in an evil, toothless smile, and he rose sluggishly and hobbled stiffly over to the boy. The Indians were oblivious to his movement as they continued their incessant chatter. He bent down, his face almost touching Billy's, his rancid breath tainting Billy's nostrils. Grabbed by panic, Billy tried to back away. Bear's hand shot out snatching Billy's hair, savagely jerking his head forward.

"You just stay right here, you slimy little bastard," the big man hissed. "The buzzards ought to be pickin' the bones of your ma and pa by now . . . that prissy, yellow-haired sister of yours, too. But don't you worry, ol' Bear saw that she got a proper fuckin' before she croaked. If it was up to me, you'd be rottin' back there with them."

Billy began to shake uncontrollably. He bit his lips until they turned white, silent tears streaming down his cheeks.

Bear whispered again, his jaw line tightening and the flesh around his eyes crimping, "You know why you're alive, you little pecker? Lone Badger just happens to have a craving for little boys—know what I mean? He's picked you out for something special. He don't have no squaw; just picks himself up a little boy once in a while . . . uses him until he gets tired of him. You're supposed to be a slave. Just you wait until we get back to the village . . . you're gonna be sleepin' with Lone Badger for a bit till he's through with you. Yes, sir, little boy," he chuckled, "that tight little ass of yours is gonna get fucked raw, and then your days are numbered."

Billy pulled away, only partially comprehending, beads of perspiration forming on his forehead. Bear released him, thumping the boy's chin sharply and ramming him forcefully against the tree. He straightened up and, unbuttoning his trousers, the giant stumbled into the woods, giggling idiotically to himself.

Later that night, Billy was jarred from his fitful sleep by a sharp kick to his buttocks. "Get your ass movin', kid," Bear growled, "Lone Badger says the raidin's done, and we're headin' for the Black Hills. Seems the folks in these parts are kinda upset, and blue bellies are gonna be coming from Fort Omaha."

In minutes, the Oglala warriors were ready to ride and led their horses into the brush on the first leg of their long journey across Nebraska to the Black Hills of southwestern South Dakota. As they departed, Billy looked forlornly over his shoulder, despair clouding his tear-filled eyes.

11

STONE DOG WASN'T anywhere in sight. He roamed far ahead of the others, trying to pick up signs of the raiders. The first several days they had followed a bloody, smoky trail across the flatlands, and Stone Dog guessed they had closed the gap to about ten hours.

As they neared the headwaters of the Little Blue, the Sioux raids seemed to peter out. Early this morning, they had paused for drinking water at a place called the Elm Creek Stockade, where a ruddy-faced man named Keeney reported that the Sioux had launched a half-hearted attack the previous afternoon. The homestead was protected by a picketed log fence some seven feet high that encompassed a large log house and outbuildings. Several families apparently occupied the tiny fortress and, upon being greeted by a rain of rifle fire, the Indians rode hastily away heading northwest, according to Keeney.

After they had retreated from the stockade, the Sioux evidently started to move at a breakneck pace. Joe pointed out that the Indians could travel for hours without food or rest, and the stamina of the smaller, lightly loaded Sioux ponies would enable them to outdistance the larger, heavier-laden mounts of their pursuers. Tom worried that their earlier gains would soon be frittered away.

It was late afternoon. A light cloud cover dimmed the sun's rays; it was cool for late August. Tom scratched the dusty, rust-colored stubble that was starting to form a healthy beard on his previously clean-shaven face. He looked over his shoulder at Joe and Sarah whose mounts plodded wearily some distance behind his own.

Joe, like the Pawnee, seemed unaffected by the grueling trek. He sat erect in his saddle, his eyes continually scanning the horizon like an eagle in search of prey. Joe was really Pawnee in spirit; strange, but Tom hadn't realized how much before. Indeed, this tough, strapping man, at this moment, looked every inch the confident, indomitable black bull for which his Pawnee brothers had named him.

Sarah never complained, but her wind-burned face was drawn, and dark circles under her eyes gave them a hollow look that vouched for her fatigue. She had become increasingly distant and remote, and her eyes had again taken on that cold, unfeeling look of their first meeting.

Tom's reasoned judgment told him they should give up the chase, but he knew he could not bring himself to suggest it. There was little doubt that Sarah would go on alone, and none of the men would turn back under those circumstances.

This afternoon, the party had ridden into rugged, hillier country again, and now they waited at the end of a deep canyon where a clear, shallow stream wound like a snake through dry, sandy grasslands bounded on each side by steep, jutting sandstone cliffs. Tom marveled at the sculpture-like formations created by nature along the face of the cliffs. Smooth, corrugated ridges that ran sideways at one point along the reddish-brown wall were so evenly spaced they reminded him of a giant washboard. Studying the sheer, canyon walls, Tom could make out a series of small cavities and niches pocking one imposing bluff at the near end of the canyon. An expansive overhang stuck out like an overhanging porch above the indentations, forming a chain of cave-like apartments about fifteen to twenty feet above the canyon floor.

Turning his eyes to the far end of the chasm, Tom could make out Stone Dog's stumpy form astride the durable paint, snaking his way hastily along the harder, rocky footing that fringed the stream. He was moving fast—too fast.

A few minutes later, as the heaving pony galloped closer, Tom read the grim look in the old Pawnee's face. Bad news.

"What's wrong, Stone Dog?" he called as the Indian approached.

"No more trail. No sign." He shook his head soberly. Then, pointing to the greenish, charcoal-colored clouds starting to roll and gyrate ominously in the west, he observed, "Bad storm."

From the unusual concern reflected in the Pawnee's single eye, Tom suspected that his comment was an understatement. "How about those caves?" he asked, pointing toward the sandstone bluffs.

"Good cover," Stone Dog replied.

"All right," Tom commanded, "let's get going." He turned his mare toward the chasm walls. Even as they neared the cliffs, a heavy drizzle drenched their shirts. Abruptly, a deafening clap of thunder echoed through the canyon, and they were engulfed by sheets of intense, driving rain. Stone Dog located a spacious rounded depression at the base of the cliffs where the horses could be secured. The travelers dismounted and unsaddled their horses, stowing their heavier gear at the deepest point of the rocky depression.

Tom led the way up a craggy, narrow ledge to a wide, flat shelf protruding from the bluff. There, they came upon a cluster of small grottoes protected by stone overhangs thrusting outward from the cliff walls above. The larger caves were four to five feet in height and several cut as deep as eight feet into the granular sandstone walls.

Sarah quickly claimed one of the narrower caves, and the men tossed their wet bedrolls and some of the food supplies in an adjacent, wider alcove.

Stone Dog and Joe clambered back down the ledge and returned shortly with armloads of soggy firewood. Tom helped Sarah build a fire in her little cave, and the other two men started a larger cooking fire in their own abode.

By this time, they were saturated, water dripping from their clothes. Tom suggested they eat before drying out for the night. Sarah, her cropped hair wet and knotted, joined her companions for a meager supper of black coffee and hardtack. They ate voraciously, and as the hot coffee did its work, Tom's spirits lifted.

He turned to Sarah, sitting apart from the others, wolfing down her rations in silence, and was struck by the misery and desolation he saw in her eyes—disturbed by the depression he felt was overtaking her. Finishing his supper, Tom suggested, "Sarah, let me take care of the cleanup. You'd better get out of those wet clothes and get dried off." Shaking her head in agreement, she slipped quietly back to her own habitation.

Stone Dog was already shedding his wet garments, and Joe and Tom joined him, stretching the drenched clothes on forked, upright sticks near the fire. Tom found a dry pair of faded denim breeches wrapped in his bedroll and pulled them on. Shirtless and barefoot, he crept closer to the fire in order to capture some of its welcome heat. With some effort, he choked back his laughter when he looked across the fire and saw his two unclothed friends sitting there like naked scarecrows, half-witted smiles spread across their sleepy, contented faces.

"Hey, Joe," he said.

The mulatto lifted his droopy head. "Yeah."

"You know, right now you look just like that expression you're always using," Tom said.

"Which one's that?"

"Pleased as a pig pissin'," Tom laughed. He ducked as a twig streaked past his ear.

As the evening wore on, the rain pounded even harder against their stony dwelling, and a tornado like wind moved in from the southwest with titanic force. The men, their backs to the wall of the cave, gazed dreamily into the fire, each lost in his own thoughts.

Finally, Tom decided he had better check on Sarah, and he crawled noiselessly out of the cave. As he crept out, he was pelted by stinging rain and hail, and he stepped swiftly along the rocky outcropping. He ducked down and squirmed into Sarah's tiny shelter, water streaming down his bare neck and back. He stopped short and started to back out when he realized that she was huddled naked in front of the fire with a gray wool blanket pulled over her shoulders and wrapped loosely about her body.

"Hello, Tom," she said softly, and motioning for him to take a place beside her, "sit down and stay awhile."

He swallowed hard when he caught a glimpse of a tender-looking pink nipple set on a firm, rounded breast. His eyes moved upward, meeting hers, and he knew instantly she had been aware of where his eyes had wandered. Tom was discomfited. He had felt like this once before when the Red Oaks cook had caught him and Joe sneaking out the kitchen door with a fresh-baked cherry pie.

Seemingly unembarrassed, Sarah pulled the blanket tighter around her body, removing further temptation from his eyes.

Tom scooted next to Sarah, not daring to look directly at her. He pretended to be entranced by the crackling, darting flames of the fire, but he was helpless to thwart an occasional glimpse of Sarah's shapely white legs out of the corners of his eyes.

After an awkward silence that seemed interminable to Tom, he turned his head slightly toward Sarah. "Are you all right, Sarah?"

She tilted her head toward his and he saw, for the first time, huge, glistening tears rolling down her cheeks, dripping onto the blanket and making widening dark splotches as they soaked in. She shivered and trembled as if her whole body had been palsy-stricken.

"Tom," she said, her haunting eyes meeting his directly, "will we find Billy?"

He hesitated only a moment and then placed his arm around her shoulders, pulling her closer to him, as he responded gently and reassuringly, "Yes, Sarah, we'll find Billy."

She leaned against him, the blanket slipping partially off her shoulders, and buried her head in the soft, sandy hair of his bare chest, her arms clenched tightly around his firm waist. She sobbed uncontrollably, almost hysterically, and he could feel the wetness spilling down his chest and belly as he was bathed by her flood of tears. A terrorizing crack of lightning reverberated off the canyon walls; she tensed and grasped him tighter. He felt the warmth and softness of her near-naked body against him, and with a terrifying sense of longing, he wanted to take her then, but he was angry at himself that the thought even found a spot in his mind after what the young woman had experienced the past few days. Instead, he tugged the blanket back around her shoulders and cradled her gently in his arms until she cried herself to sleep.

Shifting his body to lie down, but moving carefully so as not to awaken Sarah, Tom kissed her forehead lightly and stretched out next to her, enfolding her in his arms, and somehow, warm and comfortable, he easily drifted to sleep.

12

SUMMER RETURNED JUST as quickly as it had left. Green blanketed the canyon floor again, and even the fine, olive-gray buffalo grass, normally unperturbed by drought and wind, sparkled and exhibited new vigor. The sandy chasm bottom was springy and soggy, but otherwise all traces of the storm had vanished.

Saddling the horses, Tom looked over at Sarah, and she responded with an impish wink and a quick, warm smile. *My God, what now?* This was a side of her he hadn't seen before.

When he had awakened this morning, Sarah was already up and dressed and had breakfast on the fire in the larger cave. A cheerful, genial Sarah had greeted him when he stumbled in. It was almost as if she had exorcised some devil from her mind last night. She was still a headstrong, gritty, young woman, but this morning a blithe, warmhearted side of Sarah had blossomed—or come back.

Tom returned Sarah's smile. Damn, she looked almost boyish in that outfit with her short, cropped hair and the straw hat pulled down to within an inch of her eyebrows, but he knew better. What he saw was all woman.

Joe and Stone Dog were mounted. Tom's eyes caught Joe's and the latter's mouth stretched into a wide, knowing grin. Tom stepped into his saddle and edged his horse past Joe. He whispered, "You say one word, and I'll drive your grin down your throat." Joe laughed hysterically. Sarah and the Pawnee stared at Joe quizzically as Tom pushed his mare on ahead at a fast gait.

Midmorning, Tom signaled the party to a halt. While watering horses at a nearby creek, he laid out the facts. "We've lost their trail, and they're so damn far ahead of us, we'll never pick it up. We know they're likely headed for the Black Hills, and that's where we'll find Billy." For Sarah's sake he feigned confidence. "Stone Dog says we're about fifteen miles south of the Platte. We'll camp there tonight and head west along the river. The best trails follow the Platte. . . . We'll run into plenty of towns for supplies. Any questions?" For a moment he sounded like a hardheaded cavalry officer.

"No, sir, Captain, sir," Joe replied. "Troops are ready to fall in."

Tom wrinkled his forehead disgustedly, and then, much more subdued, he said, "Well, I think we'd better get going."

13

SARAH SAT LEISURELY on the soft, sandy bank of the Platte River, dangling her bare feet in the cool, slow-moving current. Dreamily, her eyes followed the graceful motions of a giant brown Sandhills crane high-stepping along the edge of a sandbar in the middle of the river, sweeping its head down intermittently to snatch an ill-fated crawdad with its long beak. Dusk was creeping in, and the last remnants of the fiery-red sun streaked through the swaying willows along the riverbank casting ghostly, oscillating shadows on the water.

Sarah started, goose bumps sprinting down her spine, when she heard a sharp snap of a twig behind her. She breathed a sigh of relief, and her lips parted in a welcoming smile when she saw it was Tom.

"Sorry, Sarah, I didn't mean to startle you," Tom said softly. "You looked so peaceful. . . . I didn't want to intrude."

"I'm glad for the company," she said. "Come and talk awhile." She patted the ground beside her. "Isn't this a beautiful river?"

"Sure is," he said. He eased down and sat cross-legged beside her. *Beautiful lady watching it, too*, he thought.

She was lovely, and he had to admit she had him totally and helplessly bewitched when she was like this.

"The river's so wide," she said, "and still. It seems almost too shallow to call a river. I waded almost to the middle a while ago, and it hardly reached my knees. It has such a flat look to it."

Tom responded, "Did you know that Nebraska was supposed to be named for this river? Somebody told me that the name comes from an Otoe Indian word 'nebrathka'—it means flat water. It crosses the whole state from east to west."

"My," she teased, "you're just a veritable fountain of knowledge. Are you sure you weren't a geography teacher instead of a soldier?"

Taking her seriously, Tom said, "I'm sorry. Joe always says I'm too professorial. He claims I'll give a lecture at the drop of a hat, says he gets his best sleep when I'm talking."

"Tom," she chided, "I was just teasing. Sometimes you take yourself too seriously." Spontaneously, she took his hand in hers and squeezed it gently, "And I love to hear you talk like this. It reveals a sensitivity you don't see in a lot of men—and I like that." Their eyes fastened, and hers said she would receive his kiss. He hesitated uncertainly and then bent toward her.

The idyllic moment was aborted curtly by a low, mournful howl from down river. Tom jumped alertly to his feet pulling Sarah up with him. His hand groped reflexively for his Peacemaker.

"That's no coyote," he whispered. "Let's get out of here."

He led Sarah hastily through the dense underbrush back toward their camp. When they bolted into camp, Tom was surprised to see Stone Dog and Joe squatting Indian fashion in front of the tiny, flickering fire, seemingly oblivious to the howling.

"All right," he said, "either you two are stone deaf, or you know something I don't know. It looks to me like you've still got ears."

Neither Joe nor Stone Dog volunteered comment.

Visibly miffed, Tom said, "Well . . . what about that phony coyote downstream? And don't tell me you don't know what the hell I'm talking about."

Joe looked like a Cheshire cat. Finally, Stone Dog said sedately, "Pawnee brothers . . . be here soon."

Suddenly, the leafy underbrush behind Joe rustled weakly and parted, and three solemn-faced Indians stepped into the clearing. Joe turned and stood up. He stepped toward the tallest of the visitors, an almond-brown man with graying, shoulder-length hair and a distinctly patrician bearing. Extending his right hand, Joe grasped the Indian's forearm firmly, and the Pawnee responded in kind.

"It has been many moons, my father."

"Yes, my son," responded the other. "The lodge of the Black Bull is too long empty."

Joe turned to Tom and Sarah. "Wolf Killer, this is my white brother, Thomas, and his woman, Sarah. We travel in search of the golden one's brother who was taken prisoner by the Sioux."

Tom flushed at Joe's references to Sarah as his woman but moved forward with her to greet the Pawnee. "Welcome to our camp, Wolf Killer. We'd be pleased to have you join us at our fire."

The Pawnee shook his head affirmatively and waved his tribesmen away. The younger, buckskin-clad Indians slipped away soundlessly into the brush.

For a moment, the Indian stared appraisingly at Sarah as if mesmerized by her brilliant, aureate hair. She smiled back, uncertainly.

Then the Pawnee fixed his eyes upon Tom. "Your woman is a daughter of the sun god. Her man will be a great warrior and gain many riches. You will have many moons together."

Embarrassed by Joe's small deception, Tom said, "I'm afraid there's a mistake, Wolf Killer. The young lady is not my wife. Joe . . . Black Bull—"

"Black Bull makes fun," said Wolf Killer knowingly. "This he is known to do. I made no fun when my words were spoken."

Darkness had settled in, and the Pawnee moved closer to the fire, squatting across the flame from Stone Dog who had remained seated like a statue. "It has been many winters, Stone Dog," said Wolf Killer.

"Many winters," the other replied.

Promptly, the two leaped into animated conversation in Pawnee dialect. Joe let himself down between the two Indians and joined the discourse only occasionally. Tom and Sarah sat apart from the others and looked on curiously.

Tom was amazed that Sarah, in light of her tragic experiences, had not been more shaken by the unexpected appearance of the Indians. She seemed not the least discomfited by the Pawnee's prophecy; neither did she appear to give it any credence. Now, her eyes were glued with fascination upon their brown-skinned guest, following his every motion, entranced by the singsong dialogue she couldn't possibly understand. She struck Tom as being unmindful of his own presence.

For several hours, the Pawnee and their black brother

palavered at the fire. Then, abruptly, Wolf Killer stood up and walked deliberately toward Tom and Sarah, who also rose as he approached.

"Your journey just begins," he said. "I do not know what you will find . . . but together, your medicine is mighty. Do not take different trails. You cannot live, Thomas, without the light of the sun." Then, his eyes falling upon Sarah, "And Sarah, the Great Spirit will take away the sun if there is no one to receive its light." The Pawnee's black eyes seemed overcome by sadness, Tom observed, and the lines that crisscrossed his noble face appeared to deepen. "We will not meet again," said Wolf Killer stoically. "I pray that the Great Spirit will be with you in the land of the Sioux dogs." He whirled around and walked out of the camp, leaving an awesome silence behind him.

An exceptional man had visited their camp that night—of that, Tom was certain. His entire manner and bearing suggested that in the white man's world, Wolf Killer would have been a general or president—perhaps a king. He had never heard much eloquence from an Indian, and his respect for the intellect of the red man, friend and foe alike, had increased immeasurably by the Pawnee's visit. The tall Indian would have made a hell of politician; he sure liked to talk in riddles.

Tom looked over at Joe. The latter's mood had seemed to grow darker and gloomier as the evening wore on, and now he gazed dejectedly into the fire. It must have something to do with what the Indian said. As usual, he could not read anything in Stone Dog's face.

Finally, he broke the stillness. "I take it our caller was an old friend of yours," Tom said. He could see that Joe was in a rare state of mind; this was a time to talk straight—no joshing.

"He's my father-in-law," said Joe. "My wife—she was killed during a Sioux raid—was Wolf Killer's only child. He has three wives, but none of them had any other children. He treated me like a son."

"He's a chief?" Tom asked.

"Yeah," Joe answered, "He's the main chief of his village . . . or he was. Wolf Killer's been on a hunting party, and now they're heading back to their village near the Loup River. By the time they get there, his people will be moving to a reservation in Oklahoma. He's going with his people, but says he'll die as soon as he gets them down there. Damn! They had a good life . . . they're good people. It's just not right."

"No," Tom agreed, "I guess we can't be very proud about the way our government's treated any of the Indians. . . . That includes the Sioux, as much as I hate their thieving hides right now. There's right and wrong on both sides of these things, I guess. Always has been, probably always will be."

Glancing uneasily at Sarah, Joe said, "We did get the lowdown on the Sioux . . . can't say it's good news, though."

"What is it?" Sarah asked worriedly.

"Well, it seems things are really stirring up Camp Robinson way. The Sioux have the Black Hills by treaty, but miners have got the gold bug, and more are moving in every day. They had an Oglala the name of Crazy Horse locked up at Camp Robinson for a while, but he's loose now, and he and Sitting Bull are out stirring up trouble. There's talk that the Sioux and Cheyenne are making big medicine in the Big Horn Mountains. According to Wolf Killer, the Seventh Cavalry is trying to take on Pawnee scouts for something big next spring. Some colonel named Custer's chompin' at the bit to take the field."

"I've heard about Custer," Tom said. "He's supposed to be a pompous ass. He was breveted a general during the Civil War when he was only twenty-three or twenty-four years old—called him the Boy General. He has a reputation for being a glory dog. Nobody questions the man's courage, but he's supposed to be as reckless as hell."

"Yeah," Joe added, "and the Sioux don't like him a bit. They call him Yellow Hair because of his long, blond hair." He smiled weakly at Sarah. "Indians are always mystical about really blond hair. Some of them think it's a gift from the Great Spirit; others just see it as a symbol of the white eyes. No matter what, it makes a lot of them nervous."

"How will this trouble affect Billy?" Sarah asked pointedly.

"Well, for one thing, we can't be sure where they're taking him; for another, they might not be so likely to keep a prisoner.... I'm sorry." The unspoken implication was clear.

Tom said, "It looks to me like we head for Camp Robinson. It's near the Black Hills and all the Sioux activity. We should be able to learn something there. I'm not as handy as you and Stone Dog on a trail, but I know how to get some answers at an army post."

"You're right," Joe said, "I think that's our starting place. We should hit North Platte by mid-morning."

Tom said, "We'll stop there and load up on supplies. We're in for a long, dusty ride through the Sandhill country these next few weeks."

14

TOM'S MOUTH WAS dry and cottony, and he ran his tongue along his cracked, parched lips. He could make out the pointed palisades of Camp Robinson in the distance. They were going to get there before sundown, and he was relieved. Even though it was mid-September, the pursuers had been baked by a blistering sun on their wearisome journey through the seemingly endless, almost monotonous, grass-shrouded mounds of sandy soil. Now the terrain was decorated with huge, isolated bluffs and rock formations rising from the earth like giant medieval castles or towers.

But the last few days had brought more than a change in scenery. As they had drawn closer to the Red Cloud Agency where Camp Robinson was located, Stone Dog had reported increasing signs of Sioux unrest. Throughout the day, they had spotted Sioux warriors on the horizon, and Tom's stomach had churned and knotted as his apprehension increased. He had mistaken the tautness and anxiety he had experienced before his first skirmish with the Sioux for symptoms of cowardice. He knew this was an affliction borne by most professional soldiers, and that the same intensity that produced the physical reaction, also cleared his mind and made him alert and ready for the battle.

He turned to Sarah who rode wearily beside him. "There it is, Sarah," he said. "With a little luck, you can scrounge up a hot bath tonight, and if Bill Jordan's still the post commander, we can look forward to a meal like you haven't had for a long time."

Tom had visited Camp Robinson on several occasions before his resignation from the army and was well acquainted with its military history. The Treaty of 1868 had guaranteed the Oglala Sioux and other bands food and supplies in exchange for lands ceded to the United States. The Red Cloud Agency was charged with issuing the goods to the Indians. Until the summer of 1873, the agency had been located on the Platte River in Wyoming, just west of the Nebraska line, and was under the nominal protection of cavalry patrols from nearby Fort Laramie. That summer, however, the agency had been moved northward to its present site on the White River in Nebraska.

Over the ensuing months, Sioux hostilities mounted until finally General Phil Sheridan ordered troops to the Red Cloud Agency. The outpost established there was named Camp Robinson in honor of Lieutenant Levi H. Robinson, who had been killed at Little Cottonwood Creek near there that winter.

Captain W.H. Jordan had been assigned to the camp as post commander in the summer of 1874, and was charged with construction of buildings and fortifications. Tom had become friendly with Captain Jordan, a seasoned veteran, when he escorted several supply trains from Fort Laramie to the camp. He recalled with relish the bountiful table set by Mrs. Jordan.

It was nearly dark when they led their tired, sweaty horses on to the camp's open parade ground. Tom had been pleasantly surprised when they were stopped at the gate by a boyish-looking corporal with a noticeable Virginia drawl. Recognizing a kinsman when Tom requested permission to enter, the youthful soldier displayed a toothy grin and signaled the party through the gates without a fuss.

Entering the wide, dusty parade ground in front of the post commander's quarters, Tom surveyed the half-completed fortress. Erection of the gate seemed an exercise in futility since the fort, still in early stages of construction, was only partially barricaded. Many of the occupants were still housed in heavy canvas wall tents positioned in straight, military rows at scattered spots throughout the fort. Still, there was little doubt that, upon completion, Camp Robinson would be a formidable military establishment. The adobe walls of the officers' quarters aligned along the north part of the encampment rested on sturdy stone foundations higher than any Tom had ever seen. The barracks, in various stages of construction, that lined the east and west sides were built of heavy log slabs, as were the warehouses and stables to the south. A cold-looking, stone guardhouse rose starkly from the south edge of the parade ground.

Tonight, the post exhibited a quiet, sleepy personality, except for an apparent hub of activity in the area of an expansive log building south and west of the military structures. From the disorderly, boisterous sounds rising from the edifice, Tom guessed this was the sutler's store-saloon.

"I'd say this is more than a camp," Joe observed.

"Yeah," Tom said, "We're going to hear a lot more about Camp Robinson before the Indian troubles are over. You've got a major fort in the making here. Hell of a lot of troops here already, too."

Tom tossed his mare's reins to Joe. "I'll check at the post commander's quarters and see if they can put us up for a few days."

He was interrupted by the hoarse, raspy voice behind him. "Good evening, gentlemen," the man said testily, "and what might you be about this evening?"

Tom turned to encounter a burly, red-faced, unmistakably Irish sergeant, who eyed the travelers suspiciously. Tom knew the type—don't give him an inch.

"Hello, Sergeant," Tom said. "My name's Tom Carnes." Gambling that Jordan was still commanding the post, he added, "I'm an old acquaintance of Captain Jordan's. I'd like to see him, if I may . . . and we're not all gentlemen here. There's a lady present."

Tom saw that the sergeant was taken aback. His orange-red, handlebar mustache twitched perceptibly. Good, he was on the defensive.

The sergeant's eyes shifted to Sarah, and his lips spread into a wide, artificial smile. "Oh, beg pardon, ma'am," he said, doffing his hat with exaggerated courtesy. Instantly, his Irish charm took over. "I think Captain Jordan's in the C.O.'s office right now. Just come along."

"Go ahead," Joe said to Tom. "We'll wait here."

Tom followed the sergeant up the steps and onto the wood porch, waiting outside as the sergeant entered the office and announced the visitor's arrival. Momentarily, the sergeant returned.

"The captain says to come on in, Mr. Carnes."

The captain, a stocky, graying man with a thick, full

mustache, rose from his desk and moved toward Tom with his hand extended as he walked into the office. "Captain Carnes," he said, "it's good to see you again."

"It's not captain anymore, sir," Tom responded, "just Tom."

"Yes, Tom, I'd heard you'd resigned your commission. You did the smart thing. It's too late for old war horses like me. I'll probably die waiting for my captain's pay clear out here to hell and gone. And promotions aren't happening these days. What can I do for you?"

Tom related the story of Billy's capture and the purpose of their visit. When he had finished, he saw kindly concern in the officer's eyes.

"I'm afraid I can't be of much help officially, Tom. We're supposed to discourage any traveling by whites into Sioux territory. You can see for yourself that something's stirring, but I can't tell you a whole lot myself. I'm an infantry officer and whatever happens is going to be the cavalry's show. Gossip is that General Crook's going to direct a campaign against the hostiles next spring . . . if Custer over at Fort Abraham Lincoln doesn't beat him to it. Anyway, you know the ropes. I'd guess your Pawnee friend will pick up more from the Indians around here in a day than you could in a week of briefings by our senior officers."

"I guess the army hasn't changed much." Tom smiled.

"No," the captain sighed, "things go slow with the army, especially promotions. Anyway, I'll inquire of our scouts and see what I can find out. Personally, I haven't heard of this Bear Jenkins and the renegades you're after. You're welcome to stay here for a few days and I'm certain you can purchase ample supplies at the sutler's store. I'll have the sergeant present the young lady to my wife, and Mrs. Jordan will see she's properly settled for the night. I have a vacancy in officers' quarters you and your other friends can occupy. Sergeant Riley," he called, "please escort the young lady to Mrs. Jordan and see that Captain Carnes and his friends are located in the vacant officers' quarters."

"Captain Carnes, sir? Uh . . . that is . . . yes, sir," the red-faced Riley answered, hustling out the door.

The captain chuckled and winked at Tom. "That's another thing about the army that never changes, Tom, you've still got to keep the non-coms guessing."

"So I've noticed," replied Tom.

Tom followed the sergeant out to the parade ground. Sarah was ushered to the captain's wife in the living area of the commanding officer's quarters. Mrs. Jordan, a plumpish, matronly woman, greeted Sarah with genuine affection and hustled her away like a mother hen that had found a lost chick.

Sarah, Tom observed, had seemed to welcome the company of the older woman. He could understand why—she had been on the trail for nearly a month with this disparate bunch.

After ordering a young private to tend to the horses, the sergeant led the men to the vacant quarters at the opposite end of a row of residences extending eastward from the Jordan quarters. He opened the door to the front room and said, "You can stay here, Mr. Carnes . . . and the nigger and Indian can bunk in the stables."

Tom flared, "The tall gentlemen's name is also Mr. Carnes." Carefully choosing his words, he added, "The other man is our good friend, Stone Dog. We'll stay together. . . . And I might remind you that your commanding officer made no such distinction in accommodations when he gave his orders. When I wore blue, sergeants got broke for disobedience."

The big sergeant's face turned beet-red, and he opened his mouth to reply, but meeting the eyes of the towering black man, thought better, did an about face, and stomped angrily away.

"Let's get cleaned up, boys," Tom said moving to the door. He paused when the Pawnee declined to follow. "Come on, Stone Dog, you'll have a soft bed tonight."

The Indian shook his head negatively. "White man's bed for women," he said disdainfully. "Stone Dog stays with Pawnee brothers." The Indian turned and traipsed across the parade grounds to join the Pawnee scouts at the stables. Tom watched the old man totter off, smiling to himself at the Pawnee's subtle insult. Shrugging, he motioned to Joe to follow him into the quarters.

The new-smelling, plastered residence afforded a welcome change. "Must be four or five rooms," Tom said as he collapsed on one of the two straw-matted bunks in the front room. "We never had it this good at Laramie."

Joe was stripping his dirty, sweat-soaked shirt when he heard a meek rapping at the door. Opening the door cautiously, he was met by a thin-boned, young private on the verge of dropping two unwieldy wooden buckets of water. The boy, dwarfed by the giant confronting him, gaped, his eyes roaming in awe over the bulging muscular arms and chest of the mulatto.

He stuttered, "C-c-compliments of Mrs. Jordan. She thought you might want to wash up and said to tell you she expects you for dinner in an hour." The towheaded private pivoted and sprinted for his barracks.

The water was more than welcome and, coming upon a bar

of lye soap near the steel wash basin provided for the quarters, the men, in turn, washed and changed. Joe trimmed his mustache and shaved the remainder of his face clean.

Tom debated shaving the curly, full beard that was forming on his face, noting, as he looked in the mirror, that somehow it aged him considerably. Deciding he wasn't up to the painful removal, he finally declined to perform the rites. Besides, there was something distinguished and mature-looking about a man with a beard.

As they left to join Captain and Mrs. Jordan for dinner, Tom was nervous and uncomfortable. Wearing only a change of creek-washed and sun-dried denims, he did not feel properly attired for the occasion, especially for a young man who, as a rising young officer, had appeared in full dress uniform at many such command performances in the past. Tonight, he would have been more at home at the enlisted men's mess.

Joe, on the other hand, seemed perfectly comfortable and needled Tom to hurry up. "Let's move," he said, "I'm so hungry, I don't care if we eat dog tonight."

They were greeted at the door by Mrs. Jordan and the cheerful, silver-haired woman promptly put Tom at ease. They were guided into the small sitting room and met by Captain Jordan, who affably offered his guests a brandy. They accepted eagerly.

Tom could hear Sarah and Mrs. Jordan chattering happily in the kitchen, and the sound of Sarah's voice made him eager to see her. Shortly, Sarah stepped lightly into the room.

"Dinner is served, gentlemen," she said breezily. "The dining room is this way."

Tom was so stunned that he shook the brandy glass at his

lips, dribbling a few drops of the brown fluid down his bearded chin. He had needed no convincing before that Sarah was a handsome woman, but tonight she was radiant—captivating. Mrs. Jordan had fitted her with a pale blue gown trimmed with white, a perfect match for those twinkling, limpid eyes. The bodice of the long dress scooped downward from the shoulders to reveal just enough of the enticing crevice of her bosom. Her hair, now somewhat longer than when she had sheared it off, was clean and shiny, like spun gold. She moved gracefully and confidently in the formal setting. Here was a woman fit to preside over a grand mansion. Damn, was this the same she-cat of a girl they found at a burning ranch not more than a month ago?

The meal was a delightful respite from the fare of recent days —roast beef, baked potatoes, fresh ear corn, topped with apple pie. It took Tom back to the days before the war. He enjoyed an update from the captain about mutual friends in the service, and as the evening wore on, he was able to glean bits of information that might serve his party in good stead in days ahead. The gracious, proper table manners of her guests belied their shabby attire, and Mrs. Jordan was enthralled with her cultured visitors and drew from Tom more information than he realized he remembered about his home in Virginia.

Sarah was effusive, and as she entered enthusiastically into the free-flowing discourse, Tom was not surprised to find that she was exceptionally well educated and informed. He learned that her mother had been a teacher in Illinois before her family came to Nebraska and was a strict taskmaster about seeing to her children's education. Tom knew his own remarks were shallow and reflected his inability to concentrate as his eyes were drawn again and again to the beautiful young woman across the table.

As the two men got up to leave, they thanked Mrs. Jordan for the fine evening and she bade them good night reluctantly. The captain produced cigars for his guests as they departed, and assured Tom again he would help them in any way he could in their quest.

Sarah joined her friends briefly on the porch. "I'd forgotten there could be times like these," she remarked to no one in particular.

"So had I," Tom answered. "So had I. It's been a long, long time."

Joe looked at his companions and smiled. "I think you two need to talk." He sauntered out on the parade ground, lighting his big cigar.

"Tom," Sarah whispered, "I hope we'll spend more evenings like this . . . together." She took his hand and squeezed it gently; he felt light-headed and his legs seemed numb and weak.

"We will, Sarah," he said softly. "I promise. We will someday."

She tilted her chin upward, and he took her tenderly, like a fragile piece of china, in his arms. Their lips touched lightly, almost timidly, rather than passionately, and when he released her, he was again overwhelmed by her quiet poise and warm, natural smile. Without a word, she pressed his hand again and whisked away quickly into the Jordans' quarters.

Tom stepped from the porch and strolled leisurely toward Joe, who was savoring his cigar and leaning drowsily against a covered Gatling gun on the parade ground. As he neared his partner, his mind was cluttered with thoughts of Sarah. *My God, what torment* . . . and then again, *what ecstasy.*

"Damn it! I've got to get hold of myself," he muttered to himself.

"What did you say, Tom?" Joe broke off his bewildered musings.

"Just talking to myself, I guess," Tom said.

"What are you so damn antsy about?" Joe asked. Then, jokingly, he added, "You act like a virgin on the verge."

Tom glared at Joe disgustedly.

With mock concern, Joe sympathized, "I'm afraid you've got a bad case, partner. That lady's got her talons stuck in you like an eagle with a rabbit. You haven't got a chance."

"What do you mean 'bad case'?" Tom responded defensively. Then, spotting a light in the sutler's store, he said, "I don't know about you, but I could stand a shot of whiskey. Come on."

Hesitating momentarily, Joe followed. "I'm not sure this is too smart, so let's make it quick."

Tom and Joe Carnes stepped casually into the dusty, smoke-filled store-saloon. An area at the far end, obviously the general store, was roped off and apparently closed for the night. At the near end was a long, ornate wooden bar that looked incongruous in the simple, rudimentary setting. The log slab wall behind the bar was adorned with stuffed deer and antelope heads. A bald, diminutive man who seemed out of place in the coarse atmosphere stood meekly behind the bar. A dozen or so small round tables were scattered haphazardly about the room and twenty to twenty-five soldiers, mostly enlisted men, played cards and swapped stories as they emptied the sutler's liquor bottles. Tom and Joe slipped as unobtrusively as possible to the bar, and the bartender, becoming fidgety, looked fearfully from side to side, and squeaked nervously, "Wh . . . what'll it be, gentlemen?"

"Two whiskeys," Joe responded.

The unrelenting din began to fade away as the bartender poured the drinks, and all of a sudden, the room was silent. The hair bristled on the back of his neck as Tom sensed the hostile tension building in the room. He could feel the eyes of the other occupants boring into his back. He caught Joe's eyes out of the corners of his own, and nodded his head imperceptibly. In unison, they downed their drinks and moved as one toward the door.

Their exodus was cut short when the burly Sergeant Riley stepped defiantly in their path. "Just one damn minute, boys," the sergeant growled drunkenly and, turning to the bartender, "Hey, Herbie. Since when did you start serving fuckin' niggers in this place?"

His face blanched white, the bartender ducked below the counter.

Wheeling back to Joe, the sergeant belched and then slurred. "And you, nigger. Who said you could drag your black ass in here?"

Tom reddened in anger and lunged toward Riley, but Joe grasped his arm firmly and pulled him back. Seemingly unflappable, Joe said, "We didn't come here looking for trouble, Sergeant. If we offended anybody, we apologize. Now, if you'll just move aside, we'll be on our way and won't trouble you any longer."

"Why you uppity, good-for-nothing son-of-a-bitch!" Riley hissed and, snatching a half-empty whisky bottle from a table, moved to strike the mulatto.

Quick as a cat, Joe's fist smashed the sergeant's wrist and the bottle slipped from his hand, shattering on the floor.

Simultaneously, he drove his knee into Riley's groin and, when the latter doubled over in agony, he brought his powerful forearm crashing down on the sergeant's neck, and the soldier crumpled like a sack of flour to the floor.

Pandemonium broke loose. Before they could reach the door, the other troopers swarmed like angered bees on Tom and Joe. Joe hoisted a puny corporal above his head and hurled him, screaming, into the mob, sending three or four others helter-skelter to the floor. Tom grabbed the chair and smashed it into the face of another charging trooper who stumbled backward out of the door, coughing uncontrollably and spitting broken teeth and blood from his mouth. Still another soldier rushed Joe, brandishing a rusty skinning knife. Joe dodged, rammed his head into the man's belly, struggling intensely with him for the weapon. When the man crawled away screaming hysterically, Joe had the knife in one hand and three of the trooper's bloody fingers in the other.

The troopers worked Joe into a corner behind the bar. Catching sight of his dilemma, Tom finished off one trooper driving his fist deep into the man's fat belly and moved to help Joe when someone hammered a table leg across the back of his skull. He reeled and pitched forward, instinctively clutching his injured head. Struggling to rise, he was conscious of warm, sticky blood oozing between his fingers before someone drove a booted foot like a sledgehammer into his groin. He was devoured by excruciating pain, fighting for breath as he heaved and retched, and then blackness overtook him, and he collapsed, unconscious, in his own vomit.

Finally, the soldiers overran Joe and pinned him to the floor, forming a human net as they sprawled over his powerful body. A drunken private slammed the heel of his boot down on the black man's head opening a vicious, jagged gash just above his eyebrow. Another pulled off his belt, looping it around Joe's neck and pulling tight.

"Let's string up the black bastard!" he yelled, and his comrades roared in agreement.

Suddenly, someone picked up the cries from outside the saloon. "Corporal of the guard. Corporal of the guard," someone called, and the warning spread like wildfire through the room.

The able-bodied, even the walking wounded, surged through the doors or bolted out the windows in their frantic efforts to escape military retribution. When a brash young lieutenant marched into the room with half a dozen uniformed troopers, only Joe and Tom and six or seven incapacitated soldiers remained. Tom and several others were carried to the guardhouse, while the others limped along behind, securely under bayonet point. There, they were deposited to spend the night on the rocky floor.

Tom regained consciousness just before daylight. Rubbing the back of his head, he ran his finger through a deep, scabby groove that split the middle of a massive lump. His right eye was swollen shut, but the former injuries were insignificant when compared to the throbbing pain radiating from between his legs. His testicles felt like they were swollen to twice their normal size, and whenever they brushed his legs, he cringed in agony.

As the feeble rays of the rising sun sifted through the barred guardhouse windows, Tom observed that Joe, too, had not come through the brawl unscathed. Ugly, raw abrasions encircled his neck and the flesh above one eye gaped open, still oozing blood that crept down the side of his swollen, bruised face.

"Well, Captain Carnes," Joe grinned weakly through puffy, disfigured lips, "and how are you this fine morning? I notice you had a good night's sleep."

Tom did not appreciate the humor, but looking around at the cell's other occupants, his spirits lifted, for he could see they hadn't fared much better.

Soon, Tom heard keys rattling outside, and, in a moment, the heavy guardhouse door inched open. "Thomas Carnes and Joseph Carnes," a stern military voice called out.

They rose, Joe helping Tom as he hobbled ever so slowly and stiffly through the door. They were escorted to the post commander's office by a seasoned, tough-looking sergeant and a youthful, smooth-faced private, and as he limped into Captain Jordan's office, Tom was surprised to find Sarah waiting in the room, dressed again in her denim riding clothes. He read no sympathy in her eyes as she glowered at him disgustedly, hands set firmly on her hips. A glance at Captain Jordan told Tom that the latter's hospitality had worn thin; abruptly, the captain confirmed his suspicions.

"Gentlemen," Captain Jordan said, "we didn't need that kind of trouble here. We extended our hospitality. In exchange, you've made a shambles of my troops. I have at least a dozen men who won't be serviceable for a week. Tom, you were an officer. You know what this kind of thing can do for the post's morale. I don't care whose fault it was, I can't tolerate these kinds of incidents. . . . And as long as the two of you are here at the fort, you'll be like a festering boil."

"Pardon me, Captain," Sarah interrupted. "What he's trying to tell us, Mr. Carnes, is that we have two hours to get our supplies, saddle up, and be out of this fort. And now, with the captain's permission, let's retire to the quarters you didn't see fit to use last night and see what I can do about patching you up." Then, turning to Captain Jordan, she said sincerely, "Thank you for your kindness and hospitality, Captain. I regret that my friends caused you this difficulty. I hope you will accept our apologies."

Tom opened his mouth in protest, but a wilting glance from Sarah cut him off.

Captain Jordan responded coolly, "I don't blame you, Miss Kesterson. It was a pleasure having you in our home. But please, get these men out of my sight as soon as possible."

Sarah turned and marched out the door. "Come on, you two," she said scornfully. Tom and Joe followed obediently like two scolded puppies.

Entering the unoccupied officers' quarters, Tom discovered that Sarah had already rounded up the salves and bandages for their medical needs. The two men sat in silence while she applied, not too gently, a foul-smelling, greasy, horse liniment to the bruises and lesions covering their faces and necks. Sarah stitched the gash above Joe's eye with surgeon like expertise, while Joe sat mutely and unflinchingly.

"Damn, your hide must be like leather," Tom said to Joe with grudging admiration. "You don't even look like you feel that needle."

Sarah whirled on him, feigning disgust, but Tom swore he caught a glint of laughter in her eyes. "I doubt if you'll be as good a patient," Sarah said, as she roughly pulled his head forward and commenced cleansing the raw wound at the base of his skull. Tom winced and pulled away.

"Ouch! Damn it. You don't need to butcher me."

"My, aren't you a baby," she chided. "If you'll hold still, I'll be done in just a minute."

As she finished bandaging a plaster like substance over the purple enclosed laceration, she said with mock innocence, "Captain Carnes, I notice that you're having extreme difficulty walking. It appears to me that you may have incurred some injuries in the lower extremities. I suggest that you drop your breeches . . . then bend over and spread your legs, so I can smear on the liniment."

Joe choked back his laughter when sharp pain bit his starchy, swollen lips.

Tom rose stiffly and awkwardly from the cot on which he was seated, and, restraining his smoldering temper, said indignantly, "I'll take care of everything else, thank you. We appreciate your help, but now I'd be grateful if you'd leave and wait outside. . . . We'll be with you in a few minutes."

She smiled mischievously, and he gingerly sat back down with dismay on the cot. Sometimes, he just didn't know how to cope with this woman. Anyway, he'd sure as hell killed his standing with her last night.

As Sarah scurried out the door, she called back, "Oh, by the way, there's a hot pot of coffee in the kitchen . . . biscuits and honey, too, if you want to eat a bite before we leave. Stone Dog's already loaded the supplies on the pack horses, and your horses should be saddled by the time you're ready. I suspect, though, you may have to ride side saddle, Captain." The door closed before Tom could reply.

Later, as they left the fort, Sarah waved goodbye to Mrs. Jordan standing on the parade ground in front of the post commander's residence, and Tom detected moistness in Sarah's eyes as they rode away. No one else seemed interested in their departure as they galloped out of Camp Robinson, Tom standing upright in his stirrups to avoid painful contact with his saddle.

They pulled up momentarily outside the fort. Stone Dog, typically, had uttered no sound to this point and cocked his head, peering quizzically at his injured comrades. Receiving no explanation, he turned to Sarah, who smiled and winked. The old Indian chuckled.

Sarah kneed her horse up next to Tom's. "Captain Carnes," she said, "I trust you are now assuming command."

Tom looked to Stone Dog. "Uh . . . I'm afraid we didn't learn much at the fort, Stone Dog. What do you think? Where do we go from here?"

Stone Dog answered simply, "Black Hills."

15

STONE DOG HAD said it was going to be an early winter, and if last night was any indication, the old Pawnee was probably right, Tom thought. It was early October, but already the nights were turning uncomfortably cold. An icy dew had settled on their blankets the previous night, and it had been late morning before the penetrating dampness evaporated from their bones. The brilliant sun was directly overhead now and scorched the back of Tom's neck, but he welcomed its warmth. That, coupled with the rhythmic plodding of the horses, made him drowsy as they made their way through brown, sun-cured grass that was almost belly high to the horses.

Glancing back over his shoulder, Tom noticed Sarah was having much the same reaction, her head bobbing sleepily, jostled by the venerable black gelding as he clomped lazily through the grass that swished like a broom against his flanks. She was tired —damned tired—he worried. She had lost weight and taken on a gaunt look since their speedy departure from Camp Robinson several weeks ago, and crimson splotches dotted her pale cheeks where they had been bitten by the whipping wind. Little streams of red branched out like spider legs from the blue irises of her eyes.

Tom and Sarah's relationship had sunk into limbo since the tender interlude at Camp Robinson. In fact, Tom didn't know where he stood with Sarah now. She'd become increasingly reticent and uncommunicative in recent days. Yes, she was congenial enough—certainly not sullen or pouty, more like preoccupied. This was understandable enough in light of their progress. They didn't seem to be any closer to finding Billy than they were a month ago. If something didn't turn up soon, they'd have to make some hard decisions about their quest. Well, he'd face that when he had to. In any case, separation from Sarah was unthinkable. He would stay the course until they had no choice but to abandon it.

The pursuers had ridden into the ashen, slate-covered mountains well over a week ago, and since then had wandered aimlessly, it seemed to Tom, over the steep, often hazardous, trails that twisted through the Black Hills. They had skirted precariously close to Oglala encampments as Stone Dog scouted for the band of Bear Jenkins. The Sioux were stirring like angry hornets. Twice, they had come upon small miners' camps to discover the mutilated handiwork of the Oglala.

Several days ago, they had stopped at a small, fortified miners' settlement called the Custer Stockade, when, at Stone Dog's suggestion, they acquired some heavy mackinaws, additional blankets, and other cold weather supplies. Tom had felt silly buying some of the items that warm afternoon, and was concerned about the added bulk for the pack animals to carry, but he remembered also that the old Pawnee hadn't been wrong very often, and he wasn't about to pull rank now.

Tom mentioned to the trader at the stockade that they were searching for some Oglala renegades that rode with a big white man.

"You're talking about Bear Jenkins," the grizzled trader had said. "If his outfit is still around here, they won't be long. They're relations of Crazy Horse's bunch, and talk is they're congregation' over Wyoming way on the Little Powder River. I tell ya, friend, if I was you, I'd get out of here like a bat out o' hell. It's gonna be mighty hot around this place for a good long spell. Shit, if the gold fever hadn't bit me, I'd ride out with ya. Army'd like to chase us all out of the hills right now."

This morning, Stone Dog had confirmed that the major Sioux villages appeared to be pulling out of the Black Hills and moving westward, probably toward the Big Horn Mountain range along the Wyoming-Montana border. There were still plenty of signs of scattered war parties, but the permanent camps were withdrawing from their sacred homeland.

Today, Stone Dog had seemed especially uneasy, fidgeting like a hound with fleas. He had ranged far ahead of the others ever since they had ridden into the open, wide-ranging valley, returning several times to his companions, circling wide to their flanks and to their rear before forging ahead again.

During one such episode, Tom queried the brown man, "Are you finding signs?"

The Pawnee answered, "Big war party," his single eye rolling skittishly from side to side.

That had been nearly an hour ago, however, and Stone Dog appeared more at ease now. Just a few moments before, he had ridden out again and now roamed far ahead, a speck on the horizon.

Tom could see that the waves of tall grasslands would soon give way to rockier, barren soil severed by deep gorges and canyons with huge granite bluffs and stark shale mountains emerging from nowhere to frame the valley's borders.

"Tom," Joe called from behind, "something's going on up there. Look at old Stony."

The urgency in Joe's voice jolted Tom from his reverie and he signaled a halt. The riders pulled up their horses, their eyes fixed on the ant-like form at the far north end of the valley. Tom could see that something was troubling the Pawnee. First, Stone Dog galloped his horse far to the right. Abruptly, he weaved to the left, and then, suddenly, to the right again. An eerie, unnatural silence permeated the valley sending shivers down Tom's spine and taking him back to an earlier time just before a Sioux ambush south of Fort Fetterman. Reflexively, he jerked his Winchester from its saddle loop; he heard Sarah's shotgun click as she shoved shells in the double chambers. Instinctively, his eyes cast about for cover in case it were needed, stopping when he spotted a cluster of stubby, granite bluffs jutting from the ground and surrounded by huge scattered boulders not more than a half mile away. His soldier's mind identified the site instantly as a natural fortress.

Suddenly, a succession of rapid popping sounds pierced the quiet, like a string of firecrackers exploding on Independence Day. The horses danced nervously, nearly throwing the riders from their saddles. Tom could barely make out tiny, filmy puffs of smoke discharging from Stone Dog's old model Winchester. Then he saw the Pawnee's horse go down, Stone Dog rolling free, and evidently tumbling into a rocky crevice off to his right.

The Sioux warriors appeared from nowhere like phantoms rising from the earth. There must have been twenty-five or thirty of them mounted on stocky, spotted ponies charging hell-bent toward the three riders. As the Sioux approached, they formed a V-shaped wedge coming to a point in the direction of Stone Dog's dead horse.

Tom spun his horse around, and reined up short. His first instinct had been to retreat blindly for the open end of the V. Too damn easy, he thought, and turned the mare toward the rocky buttes lying beyond the left wing of the charging Indians.

"Come on," Tom yelled, "ride like hell!"

"But Tom," Sarah protested, "they're coming right at us."

Tom yanked his saber free from the bedroll behind his saddle and snapped, "Sarah, for Christ's sake. For once, shut up and do what you're told." He flourished his saber in the air and charged recklessly, like a man possessed, toward the line of approaching Oglala. His companions wavered and then fell in behind.

The stunned Indians pulled up their ponies and froze momentarily, apparently taken aback at the audacity of the charging band. Before the Sioux could renew their attack, the riders were upon them. One brawny-shouldered buck, war axe uplifted, drove his pony into Tom's mount, threatening to topple the struggling mare. Without warning, Tom's gleaming saber swept downward, its driving force slashing like a guillotine into the Indian's neck, and the Oglala pitched from his pony, his severed head flopping lifelessly against blood-drenched shoulders. Joe's pistol cracked and another warrior plunged forward, red fluid spewing from the gaping hole that had been his nose.

Forcing his way through the Oglala ranks that had been thinned in formation of the wedge, Tom stabbed and slashed, his arm swinging like a well-oiled machine, until he broke into the clear, Joe and Sarah crowding his flanks. Instantly, they bolted, frantically and resolutely toward the buttes, but not before the pack animals were yanked loose by a Sioux warrior.

The Indians chased after them in frenzied pursuit, their incensed, blood-curdling cries ringing through the basin.

Tom noted that few shots had been fired by the Oglala in the onslaught, and deduced that they had few firearms. No sooner had he made that observation, than a rifle cracked and his mare faltered and lurched forward, stumbling to the grassy earth, blood seeping from her neck. Tom leaped free of the horse as Sarah and Joe tore past. Throwing himself behind the dying mare, he fired three quick shots with his Winchester, slowing the rush of the Sioux momentarily. In the meantime, Joe and Sarah had swung around, and Sarah veered her horse toward Tom as Joe's Peacemaker kept the Indians at bay. As she reached Tom, Sarah stretched out her hand and Tom seized it firmly, pulling himself up behind her on the black gelding. In a few seconds, they were racing again toward the rock fortress, Joe stopping and whirling intermittently to fire a volley of shots at the oncoming Oglala, slowing them just enough to enable him and his friends to maintain their slim lead.

As they reached the stone-belted bluffs, Tom slid from the horse, taking cover behind a jagged granite boulder and unloosing a rain of rifle fire at the Oglala until Joe scrambled into the rock sanctuary. As Sarah tethered the horses, the two men served the Indians a torrent of bullets, and, finally, the attackers eased away from the rocks to regroup out of gunfire range.

Casting about for better cover, Tom saw that the Indians' main effort would have to be directed toward frontal attack. He had indeed selected a natural fortress—their rear was protected by a steep, craggy bluff, perhaps forty feet at its highest point, and stretching not less than one hundred feet from north to south, its ends curving outward to form a crescent-shaped formation with the defenders cradled midway in the concave. Just behind his party, Tom noticed that a segment of the cliff rose some five feet from the earth and cut back into the bluff another ten feet or so before the sheer walls rose to meet the sky. The rock platform seemed almost stage-like as its sides narrowed gradually to meet the stark cliff walls. Several giant boulders, one taller than Joe, protected the outer edge of the shelf.

"Get everything up on that ledge," Tom ordered, gesturing toward the escarpment. "Joe, this bunch must be hard up for guns. There couldn't have been more than half a dozen rifles firing out there. The height we can get from that ledge should help us even things up a bit when they charge again. We need to get some more cover up there, though . . . and fast."

Instantly, the men went to work hoisting large stones up onto the shelf. Sarah rolled the boulders into strategic places plugging several gaping holes with the two remaining saddles. In a short time, they fashioned a crude barricade forming a pocket of protection for the defenders that looked like a mammoth swallow's nest plastered against the cliff's face.

Inventorying their depleted arsenal, Tom tallied only the Winchesters and pistols of the two men, his own saber, and Sarah's double-barreled shotgun. Sarah had carried her shotgun shells in her saddle bag, so she had ample ammunition, but the shotgun was only effective at close range. There were enough .44 cartridges for perhaps eighty rounds each for Tom and Joe, but unless the Sioux discouraged easily, it wouldn't be enough. The water situation was even more ominous. They could make it last two days if they rationed it sparingly, he reasoned, and becoming aware for the first time of his sweat-sopped shirt and the perspiration dripping off his beard, he added, if they were lucky. There sure as hell wouldn't be any food—that got away with the pack horses.

The defenders perched themselves on the iron-hard shelf, Joe positioning himself belly-down behind one of the saddles lodged firmly between two shale slabs. Tom directed Sarah to their far left flank, the lowest point on the ledge where the Indians would be most likely to make an assault in an attempt to overrun the barricade. It bothered him to place her at such a vulnerable spot, but he knew that was where the shotgun would inflict the most damage. Sarah obeyed unquestioningly and only the frantic caged-animal look in her eyes betrayed her fear. She had said hardly a word, only a polite 'yes' or 'no' since Tom's earlier sharp reprimand.

Tom bent down to counsel with Joe. Before he could speak, Joe whispered, "She's one hell of a gutsy lady, isn't she, partner?"

Tom responded with a single affirmative nod before changing the subject, "What in the hell are they doing out there?"

Tom calculated that it had been nearly two hours since they took refuge in the bluffs. Unless the Sioux were settling in for a prolonged siege, he could not understand why they had given the defenders time to entrench themselves. Crazy Horse would have regrouped his Oglala and overrun Tom's little band instantly. It was evident that the leader of this war party was less decisive.

Peering over the crude barricade, Tom observed a whirling cloud of smoke like dust moving rapidly from the area where he had last seen Stone Dog toward the main body of the Oglala. Shortly, another dozen warriors joined those beyond the bluffs, several talking animatedly and pointing in the direction from which they had come. Suddenly, Tom understood why the Indians had not attacked. One of the new arrivals was apparently the leader of the war party—likely, one of the bunch that had been waiting ahead in ambush when spotted by Stone Dog. Poor old Stony, they must have been finishing him off.

Tom fixed his eyes on the Sioux leader. Considerably taller than the average Oglala, he clearly had what the military called "presence of command." The Indian, a young man with braided, black hair, waved his arms and rode back and forth in front of his tribesman, looking in the direction of the bluff, searching for his enemies' weaknesses. Tom knew this had to be a full-fledged war party, blood hungry and impatient for the kill. Common sense told him that Indians in this mood would not willingly suffer a protracted battle. The leader would want to deal the death blow quickly and be on his way. Neither would he wish to incur infinite losses for so small a prize, Tom suspected. If they could just hold out long enough, there was at least some small hope the Sioux would move on. It was already late afternoon; perhaps, if they could survive till nightfall.

The tall warrior lifted his right arm, waving it first to the left and then to the right, and the Indians fanned out in a single line forming a semicircle on the flatlands, something over one hundred yards in front of the rocky breastworks. Damn good strategy, Tom thought grudgingly. If the Oglala came in a bunch, they could shoot in a crowd and have a good chance of hitting somebody. This way, they would have to pick the Sioux off one at a time.

Tom rose and moved off to Joe's right to the highest point of the ledge, spotting himself behind one of the giant boulders. He leveled his Winchester across a ragged niche in the granite and waited.

The Oglala sat on their motionless ponies like statues on the horizon, eyes focused vulture-like on their besieged enemies. Not more than four or five, including the leader, were armed with rifles. Some carried short bows, most already strung with feathered arrows, and others displayed long, wicked-looking lances held upright in their hands. At the sight of the lances, Tom shuddered, recalling bizarre scenes from earlier days on the frontier. He had always thought that death by a bullet was many times preferable to that of a spear.

Tom tossed a glance at Sarah. The tension showed in the tightness of her jaw and the grimness of her mouth. "Just a little delay, Sarah," he said easily. "Don't worry. Just take it easy and do your job. We can hold them off. I don't think these birds want to pay the price."

She relaxed noticeably, and, with a feeble, nervous smile, patted her shotgun to indicate her readiness.

The Oglala leader flourished his rifle signaling the attack and, like a single, orchestrated wave, they swept toward the bluff.

"Wait till they're closer," Tom cautioned, as the Indians charged nearer, their frenzied whoops increasing in intensity, almost drawing even Tom, with his military patience, to commence premature firing, but he held back. Then, after a few moments, "Okay . . . now!"

The two Winchesters cracked again and again as the Indians approached the scattered boulders in front of the bluff. Three Indians tumbled from their horses, and another wheeled his spotted pony in retreat, blood running freely down his side, painting his body scarlet. A shower of arrows bounced against the barricade and the rocky cliff face behind. As the defenders ducked to elude the barbed onslaught, half a dozen warriors leaped from their ponies, rolling behind the meager shelter of rocks beneath the rampart. With this accomplished, the main body swung away from the bluffs, racing back to regroup, but not before Joe slammed another bullet into the neck of a fleeing warrior.

Tom breathed a sigh of relief at the brief respite, and the two men snapped cartridges into their Winchesters, readying for their next assault. The roar of Sarah's shotgun broke the stillness, as an Indian, climbing up the embattled scarp toppled backward, his chest a bloody mass. A rifle exploded from below, and a bullet chipped the rock just left of Tom's ear. He ducked, aware, for the first time, of the attackers below.

"There're at least four or five down here," Sarah called to Tom. "A couple of them have rifles. It looks like the others are supposed to rush us."

"They have to come in by your side," Tom answered, wiping the stinging sweat from his eyes. "Can you handle it over there?"

"You're damned right, I can," she said slamming a shell into her shotgun's empty chamber, "but don't let any more of them get down here."

Sarah's fear had evaporated. The waiting was the worst part, and that was over. She'd do.

Properly reprimanded, Tom leveled a shot at an Indian

skulking in the rocks below; a sharp yelp indicated that he drew blood.

"Here come the bastards!" Joe yelled as dust rolled from under the thumping hooves of the advancing ponies.

Two more Oglala fell, mortally wounded, before arrows rained again like large hailstones against the rocky fortress, but, before the Indians rode away from the bluff, Tom caught sight of several more slipping behind the rocks below.

"They're in a hurry, Joe," said Tom, "and the only way they can get this job done before nightfall is to overrun us. Keep your eyes on the low side. I think Sarah's going to need help on the next charge."

No sooner had his words escaped, than the main body rumbled in again toward the bluffs. Simultaneously, the others leaped up from behind the rocks and rushed toward the ledge. Tom's Winchester cracked and another Indian pitched backward, clutching his forehead as he struck the ground, his legs kicking convulsively.

Others reached the wall below the ledge, however, and hugged tight against it, out of reach of the rifle fire. Twice, Sarah's shotgun thundered, and Joe jumped to her aid as he saw a bare-chested Sioux warrior, his face a crimson, pulpy mass, release his hold on the stone shelf, and fall backward bowling over several of his red brothers as his body crashed to the earth. Sarah crouched against the cliff wall, fumbling with the shells as she hurried to reload the double chambers. A skinny warrior pulled himself upon the ledge, pushing away several of the big rocks that formed the barrier. Spying Sarah, he raised his war club to strike, but the weapon dropped in midair when Joe's Winchester bullet ripped through his belly. The Indian plunged forward, hitting Sarah sharply as he fell, jarring the shotgun from her hands. As she leaped for the shotgun, two more warriors climbed over the ledge, one brandishing a wicked, steel war axe, and the other lifting a sharp, stake-like lance behind him. Joe's rifle jammed as he squeezed the trigger and, whipping it around, he grabbed the barrel end and drove the Winchester's butt into the head of the axe bearer. Sarah retrieved her shotgun just as a third Indian gained footing on the ledge, and, from a sitting position, pulled the trigger blasting the Indian in the groin and sending him, shrieking, backward to the ground below.

Tom was oblivious to the bloody struggle around him as he held the outlying Oglala at bay with steady fire, and he never saw the Indian that drove the lance deep into his muscled back just under the right should blade. Dark blood soaked his shirt; abrupt searing pain swept Tom's back. His arms tensed and stiffened, and the rifle dropped uncontrollably from his hands. He felt overwhelming nausea and dizziness before he crumpled to the ledge and everything went black.

Sarah paled when she saw Tom sink, with the lance sticking grotesquely from his back and crimson spreading over his denim shirt. But, before the Indian could withdraw the lance, she emptied the shotgun's second chamber broadside in his chest. Stunned, she threw the gun aside, and moved to Tom, glancing momentarily at the dying Indian sitting with his back against the face of the cliff. She received an almost sadistic pleasure when the urine ran down his legs and his bowels emptied, as he flopped forward in death.

Joe, in the meantime, snatched up Tom's Winchester and braced himself like an enraged Goliath to drive the invaders from their sanctuary. But to his surprise, no one came to face his wrath.

Then, he paused, hearing an almost rhythmic snapping of rifle fire from the far end of the butte and to the left of the attackers. He caught the glint of sun against metal about half way up the face of the bluff, and, over the remnants of the barricade, he saw the Indians pointing excitedly toward the sniper as bullets sprayed about them. The mounted warriors had already eased away from the bluff and retreated beyond rifle range, and now, the few remaining in the rocks below took off like rabbits, streaking frantically toward the main body. Joe let loose a few token shots at the escaping Indians and then whirled to help Sarah.

She had just pulled the bloodied lance from Tom's back, and blood gurgled and bubbled from the puckered hole like lava from a seething volcano. Sarah slashed away his shirt, wadding some of the pieces into a ball and jamming it into the bloody chasm, pressing firmly as scarlet fluid trickled out around it.

"Jesus Christ, look at that mess," murmured Joe as he knelt beside Tom's still body. His eyes met Sarah's for a second, and he saw heart-sinking despair there, as big, silent tears rolled slowly down her cheeks, streaking her dust-caked face.

"Joe, help me drag him back in the shade," she said.

Joe did not hear; he just stared at Tom's back as the blood from the awful wound saturated the crude compress and seeped up between Sarah's fingers.

"Joe, damn it! I said help me move him," she said sharply.

Shocked by the harshness in her voice, Joe obeyed and moved to assist, pausing just briefly to look over the barrier to be certain the Indians were staying put.

"It's bad, Sarah . . . real bad . . . the worst I've ever seen."

Shaking his head helplessly, tears starting to well now from his dark eyes, he choked, "He's my brother, Sarah. Did you know that? He's my brother . . . we had the same papa."

Sarah shredded some more of Tom's shirt making a new compress from the dirty rags. "Joe, wet a few of these rags for me. I've got to clean around here and see what we've got. He's going to live . . . he's got to live," she said determinedly. "He said he'd help me find Billy . . . he promised . . . he promised, and . . . oh, God, I love him, Joe."

Rocks rattled as they struck the ground below and Joe, abruptly brought to his senses, grabbed for his rifle as a brown hand reached over the ledge.

"Hot as white man's hell," Stone Dog grumbled, as the ugly little man pulled himself upon the ledge and stepped nonchalantly into the tiny parapet, spitting a wad of tobacco back over the side. Then, seeing the prone, silent figure stretched out on the rock floor, the Pawnee moved catlike to Sarah's side. The old Indian pulled back the sopped, red compress and studied the gory cavity in Tom's back. "Damn bad," he mumbled. "Big damn bad." Then, catching Sarah's anguish, he reached out and patted her shoulder gravely.

"They're pulling out," Joe yelled jubilantly. "The dirty bastards are pulling out!"

Stone Dog joined him at the barricade briefly, and, sure enough, saw the Oglala ponies racing away, fading quickly out of sight.

"They almost had us," Joe said. "Why are they quitting now?"

"Almost dark. Cost too many warriors. Many Oglala heading for Powder River country," Stone Dog commented solemnly.

Then the two men turned to their fallen comrade.

16

THE NIGHT'S CHILL was already settling in, even before the flaming orange of the sun disappeared over the horizon. Sarah's fingers touched the back of Tom's neck and a worried frown crept over her face as she felt the unhealthy, fiery heat emanating from his skin. Stone Dog had left briefly and returned a short time ago with an assortment of plants and herbs, which he had ground patiently between stones and then mixed with water and boiled over their small fire until he had a greenish, putrid-smelling gumbo. This he had stuffed deep into Tom's wound and then asked Sarah to prepare another compress, which they bound tightly around Tom's back and across his chest with long strips of cloth torn from Joe's shirt.

Hot as he appeared to be, Tom began to shiver and tremble from the combined effects of fever and the nipping mountain air. Sarah could see the scarlet tentacles of fevered flesh spreading out from beneath the bandages, and knew that the anticipated infection had announced its arrival. She slipped her fingers to the crusty red-brown rags covering the wound and traced the rising, bulging tissues there.

Joe and Stone Dog had taken inventory of their few remaining supplies. Joe's horse had taken a bullet during one of the Sioux assaults and among them, they now had one mount, Sarah's ornery black gelding. Stone Dog had been able to salvage a few blankets and coats from his and Tom's dead horses, which the Sioux had apparently overlooked in their eagerness to depart. Food supplies had disappeared with the pack horses, and the party would have to rely on Stone Dog and Joe to locate and kill wild game. If they had horses, Tom still could not be transported, even by travois, since the slightest movement triggered a new flow of blood from the pit in his back.

Using one of the retrieved blankets and some slender poles, the men had constructed a makeshift lean-to shelter above Tom's place on the ledge. Sarah had moved her few remaining belongings and bedroll into the small refuge beside Tom, while Joe and the Pawnee tossed their makeshift bedding at the base of the butte, just beneath the ledge.

Sarah spun with a start as Joe lifted himself upon the ledge, sending a few small stones clattering to the rocky ground below. "He's burning up, Joe," she said matter-of-factly, "but I don't know what else we can do for him."

"Nothing, Sarah," he responded. "Stone Dog says we just wait. We've been talking things over. . . . Whether Tom lives or dies, we're going to need horses and supplies before we move on. If he makes it," he said soberly, "it'll be days, maybe even weeks, before we can ride. We've agreed I should take the horse and go back to Custer Stockade or find some other place to re-supply. With luck, I can be back here in a few days. Stone Dog will stay here with you and Tom. He can help Tom more than I can, and he has a better chance of keeping you alive in his place if I don't make it back. Sound okay?"

"Sounds okay," she answered softly. She took his huge, rough hand in hers and squeezed it comfortingly. "And thanks, Joe. . . . Thanks for everything. We'll bring him through this," she said adamantly. "I guarantee it. Then we'll find Billy."

He smiled uncertainly. "If you say so, Sarah, I believe it. Now, I think I'll get some shut-eye. It's been kind of a long day, and I want to pull out first thing in the morning. Stone Dog says he'll check on Tom every few hours. If you need us before, just holler."

She released his hand, "Good night, Joe."

It was dark now. Sarah gazed into the black sky, speckled this clear, crisp night with millions of glittering stars. She picked out the Big Dipper, and, tracing along the two stars in the front of the cup, as she had been so carefully taught by Sam Kesterson, she spotted the North Star. She bowed her head and sat there silently, and then, wiping the warm dampness from the corners of her eyes, she crawled under the blanket next to Tom, pressing close to his trembling body in an effort to protect it from the night's chill. In a few moments, she dozed off, her arm stretched limply across the small of his back, her head nestled next to his heaving ribs.

17

THE SIOUX BAND edged their ponies up the rugged shale incline. Less than ten feet to his right, Billy could see that the rock terminated abruptly, dropping off to form a sheer cliff that stretched some three hundred feet below to a narrow, pine-covered plateau running the length of the cliff. The plateau ended at a rocky rim supported by steep granite walls that dropped still farther into an enormous, seemingly endless, canyon. Billy could make out the blue-white ribbon of a creek that roared and twisted its way through the rocky canyon floor. He could hear the clanking of metal against rock echoing through the canyon walls below, and he observed three or four distinct streams of gray, powdery smoke rising up from the chasm bottom. Dozens of ant-like figures scurried back and forth along the banks of the creek.

Bear and his band had kept their distance from the canyon. Bear had told Lone Badger earlier, "We ain't takin' on no miners today. We gotta get back to the village and find out what's goin' on in these hills."

Ever since he overheard that conversation, Billy's eyes had

been fixed forlornly on the activity in the canyon below. Several days before, Bear had warned Billy, in his peculiarly vulgar way, that the boy would get his comeuppance soon. And, just yesterday, Billy had first sighted the gray-black outline of the mountains they had now entered. Even a small boy could conclude that these were surely the Black Hills, and the men below were, no doubt, miners armed and ready for a fight.

Billy's attention was diverted abruptly from the canyon, by the harsh, painful rapping of a rifle barrel against his already tender, bruised ribs. "Okay, you puny little bastard," Bear whispered knowingly, "just keep your eyes up front. You ain't going down there. Tomorrow night, this little trip will be over, and you'll be all bedded in with Lone Badger." He grinned evilly, running his tongue along his broken teeth, and then, choking a bit, foamy saliva flecked with brown bits of tobacco rolled out of the corner of his mouth.

Billy shivered involuntarily and then, for just a moment cast his eyes again, miserably, down the canyon.

18

THERE WAS A new enthusiasm in the camp. The night was pitch black, and a frosty wind nipped at Billy's nose and ears as he huddled near the fire, a tattered wool blanket pulled over his shoulders. Normally, the camp would have been asleep by this time, but the warriors chattered excitedly, obviously anticipating their arrival the next day at the main camp. Billy sat across the fire from Bear and Lone Badger who were arguing vociferously.

"Goddamn it, Lone Badger," Bear said, "these boys is gonna be madder than hell if the village is already moved out. We lost two . . . maybe three . . . weeks 'cause you got a hair up your ass and had to go on another raidin' streak. Well, shit! My ass is gettin' saddle sore, and I ain't in no mood to follow a bunch of crazy Oglala into the Big Horns . . . least ways, not till I stuffed my belly and shacked up with my squaw a mite. Christ, it's October; it could be snowin' and cold as hell by the time we'd hit the Big Horns."

Lone Badger spat, "Bear does not have to follow Oglala leader. Can go back to white eyes friends if he wants." He slipped out his blood-crusted scalping knife and glared at Bear.

"No more back talk."

Bear scratched his rump. "Aw, shit," he said. "I didn't mean nothin'."

Lone Badger hadn't touched Billy for days, but Billy was startled, almost frightened, just a short time earlier this evening when the warrior had stooped and again started kneading his buttocks, and then, suddenly, had forced his hands into Billy's breeches and tugged roughly at his genitals. Terror-stricken, Billy had squirmed away. Upon removing his hand, the Sioux had scratched at his own groin, grinning wickedly, and Billy's eyes had opened wide in alarm when the Indian's stiff, swollen organ popped inadvertently from the side of his breechclout. Bear, observing the incident as he gummed his supper a short distance away, had roared convulsively, stopping instantly, almost choking on his own saliva, when his eyes met Lone Badger's icy glare.

After Lone Badger had stomped away, Bear chortled, "He's just getting warmed up, little fella. You behave yourself, and that old Injun will give you a taste of that hunk of meat in his britches. Just you wait till tomorrow night. . . . Boy, would I like to have me a little peephole," he giggled. "And then, in a few weeks, when that old buck's through with ya, you're gonna come visit ol' Bear for a few days . . . 'fore we cut your balls off."

Billy shuddered. Since Billy had quit resisting, his hands and feet had been bound only while the Indians slept at night. During the day and early evening, he was free to wander about as long as he did not leave the sight of the others. He was expected to gather wood and perform other menial tasks, but beyond that, he had been virtually ignored by all except Bear and Lone Badger.

Ever since he had seen the miners in the canyon, Billy's

spirits had buoyed with thoughts that he may have found a way to escape his dilemma. In the background now, he could hear the monotonous hum of a little stream splashing over the rocks down the steep mountainside that sloped away from the Sioux camp.

His father had once told him, "Billy, if you are ever lost, find the nearest stream. That stream will eventually lead you to a creek, and the creek will flow into a river. The river will finally take you to people." The cold stream meandered back in the direction they had come from, and would take him to the miners or other white people—if he could get that far.

Billy rose slowly from his place by the fire, letting the blanket fall from his shoulders and drop in a heap on the ground. Lone Badger was talking to another warrior at the next fire; Bear, sitting across from Billy, eyed him suspiciously. Billy commenced unbuttoning his trousers and walked casually into the timber as if he were going to relieve himself. Bear's eyes bored after him, but the big man did not attempt to follow.

Once hidden by the pine, Billy did not bother to look back but raced full speed toward the humming sound ahead of him. Upon reaching the stream, he dashed along its rocky banks down the chiseled mountainside, following the course of the stream. Once he stumbled and rolled some twenty feet down the precipitous incline coming to rest sharply against a ponderosa. Another time, he slipped on the sliding shale, and jumped up, only to step off a ten-foot embankment, dropping with a thud to the hard granite floor below. When he struggled up, a sickening pain ripped through his right knee, and he limped noticeably as he charged on ahead.

The terrain became increasingly steep and rugged as Billy

made his way down the slope, and now the stream cascaded down the mountain over a series of small falls, perhaps three or four feet in height. Billy stopped momentarily, catching his breath and rubbing his knee vigorously where it had begun to stiffen. He bolted upright when he heard rocks and shale rattling upstream behind him, signaling that his escape had been discovered. Panic-stricken, he ran blindly and recklessly down the slope, sliding and rolling almost as much as he walked. The pain in his knee intensified, and, soon, he was hobbling along, giving ground quickly to his relentless pursuers.

"There's the little son-of-a-bitch," Bear roared, and Billy could make out the dark outline of the hulking figure not more than a hundred feet up the mountainside.

One of the Sioux was loping along at the side of the huge man and leaped ahead, like a mountain lion moving for the kill, when he saw Billy. At the sight of the Indian racing toward him, Billy jumped, feet first, into the icy stream. The torrential water, though only several feet in depth, lifted him like a twig and sent him shooting down the mountainside, bouncing over one small fall and then another. Billy gasped for breath and floundered like a turtle on its back, attempting to regain his balance as the stream's force swept him farther down the mountainside, leaving his pursuers far behind.

Finally, the water began to slow and the falls became less frequent, their drop smaller, until shortly, it almost leveled out. Billy reached out and snagged a limb of an overhanging pine and pulled himself, shivering, from the water, collapsing in exhaustion upon the shale bank. Numbness crept into his feet and hands, and an overpowering drowsiness started to overtake him, but the heightened pain radiating from his knee snapped him back to consciousness, and he staggered up to continue his flight downstream—away from Bear's smelly mouth, away from Lone Badger's probing hands.

The grade was gradual now, and Billy shuffled along the edge of the widening stream, halting momentarily upon hearing a louder, steady roar of water ahead. Quickening his pace, in a short time, Billy limped out on the floor of an immense, broad canyon, and he took on a new burst of energy when he saw his friendly stream emptying into the large, raging creek that foamed and raced along the canyon floor.

Angling away from the stream, he followed the turbulent waters on their twisting journey through the canyon. For hours, Billy stumbled along the creek's shale bank, oblivious to the ghostly whistling of the wind as it tore through the ever-narrowing canyon, and unaware of the eerie shadows cast along the chasm bottom by the towering, jagged canyon walls.

Finally, the pulsating pain in his knee became unbearable and the tremors vibrating through his body became unstoppable. He paused and bent over to catch his breath, took a few more steps, and then he tumbled face down to the canyon floor. Drawing his arms up and under his head, he closed his eyes and fell into a fevered sleep.

19

"GODDAMN IT, LUCY, will you stop that God-awful bawling? It ain't time to go to work yet," yelled the grizzled old miner.

"Crawdad, if you don't shut that burro up, I'm gonna have donkey meat for supper," came a voice from a makeshift canvas tent farther downstream.

"Well, don't crap your pants. I'll take care of her," grumbled Crawdad Logan as the balding, gray-bearded man stomped toward the braying burro about a hundred yards upstream. Mumbling to himself and rubbing his sore, stiff back as he neared the old jenny, Crawdad habitually searched the brush for signs of Sioux.

Lucy had to be nearly twenty years old. She had always been an obstinate beast, but she did not usually raise a ruckus without reason. "You wanna be buzzard bait?" he scolded the old burro as he came up beside her. Lucy cocked her head and, looking at the miner contemptuously, threw her long ears back and brayed loudly.

"Damn you." The old man raised his fist threateningly. Then, spotting the silent, dirty figure sprawled between the rocks not more than ten feet in front of the burro, he exclaimed, "What in the hell—"

Crawdad hobbled over to Billy's still form and rolled him over, running his gnarled hands over the boy's face and chest, seeking signs of life. He felt the gentle rise and fall beneath Billy's bony ribs, and shook his shoulders in an effort to bring him to consciousness but got no response. He lifted the boy in his hard, strong arms and staggered back toward camp, yelling, "Jasper! Get some blankets and get the damn fire goin'. We got us a visitor."

Jasper Johnson, a tall, stringy young man, tossed some axe-hewn pine boughs on the red-hot embers left from the previous night's fire. In a few moments, a crackling, orange flame crawled up the logs and commenced to remove the chill from the frosty morning air.

Crawdad placed Billy next to the fire, and Jasper moved to help him remove the boy's water-soaked clothes. Then they wrapped Billy in scratchy wool blankets, rubbing his hands and feet vigorously as they dragged him still closer to the fire.

Jasper, a beardless man, with a cherub like face, asked, "Where'd he come from, Crawdad?"

"How in the hell would I know," muttered the other testily. "He's in a hell of a shape, that's for sure."

In the meantime, the camp had come alive and other miners, as many as twenty, gathered about the fire to satisfy their curiosity. When Billy failed to respond to Crawdad's ministrations, the old miner was showered with a barrage of unsolicited medical advice.

An unreceptive Crawdad finally stood up and glowered at this audience. "If I want your help, I'll let you know," he said.

"Now this here's a mighty sick young feller, but your standing here gawkin' at him sure as hell ain't gonna make him any better . . . so git." The crowd broke up slowly, and the men shuffled away reluctantly, grumbling as they moved back to their own campsites.

Crawdad and Jasper remained at Billy's side and finally, as the warm rays of the morning sun drifted over the canyon walls, Crawdad noticed that some of the blue was fading from the boy's ankles and wrists, and a tinge of pink was returning to his ghostly white cheeks.

Shortly, Billy's eyelids fluttered, and his eyes popped open. Slowly, he turned his head, looking blankly at the faces of the two miners. Then, with a weak smile, he said hesitantly in a soft, squeaky voice, "I'm Billy Kesterson. . . . I must have got away from the Indians."

For the first time, Crawdad laughed. "You sure did, sonny, you sure as hell did."

20

"LOOK AT THAT swelling," Sarah pointed out unnecessarily to the grim-faced Stone Dog. She ran her fingers lightly over the hideous lump that ballooned out around the tight bandages to expose the brown, clotted wound; she winced. "The infection must be terrible. It's puffed up twice as big as yesterday, and look . . . it's turning black and yellowish around the opening."

It was midday, but Sarah shivered from the cold as a brisk wind nipped around her shoulders and steel-gray clouds hovered over her head blocking the sun's warmth. But in spite of the coolness of the day, big droplets of sweat rolled off Tom's neck and back, and he seemed decidedly weaker. The only encouraging signs since Joe's departure the previous morning were intermittent intervals of semi-consciousness when Tom would interlace incoherent ramblings with nightmarish screaming and then fade again into oblivion. During those periods, Sarah had successfully forced him to swallow small amounts of water to help replenish his dwindling body fluids.

Now, Sarah and Stone Dog cleansed the ugly flesh around the wound. According to Stone Dog, the blood that oozed from the crater like wound was no longer a real threat to Tom's life; he was not going to bleed to death. The infection was another matter, however. If the fever didn't break, and if Tom didn't take some nourishment, his string would run out soon. Sarah looked at the old Pawnee. "Feel the softness of the swelling, Stone Dog. It has to be full of pus and fluid. If we can't do something about it, the infection's going to spread through his whole body."

"Need to cut out poison," Stone Dog nodded solemnly. He stretched out his hand, gesturing for Sarah's hunting knife. Squatting by the fire, the Indian held the blade near the coals until the razor-sharp edge was red-hot. Then, straddling Tom's back, he pushed the keen point abruptly into the depths of the wound. As the knife pierced the scabby seal, yellow, brownish fluid gushed suddenly from the crevice, and Sarah gagged momentarily when the putrid gas struck her nostrils, causing vomit to rise in her throat. His face impassive, the Pawnee sliced at the rank flesh encircling the wound and, as he probed deeper, chunks of pus, the texture of curdled milk, intermingled with red, fresh blood, flowed from the incision. The Indian scraped and scooped the foul matter from the cavity, hacking away small bits of gangrenous flesh near the surface as he worked.

When he had finished, the swollen mass was totally deflated, leaving a huge indentation in Tom's back, centered by a huge, puckered hole large enough to receive a man's fist. Sarah packed the wound with Stone Dog's Pawnee medicine and then redressed it.

"Now we wait," said Stone Dog. He walked away and climbed down the ledge, leaving Sarah to her lonely, silent vigil.

Tom's rasping, labored breathing eased almost instantly after Stone dog lanced the awful wound, but when nightfall set in, there were still no signs that his fever had broken. Worse yet, Tom had had no further moments of consciousness.

Just before sunrise the following morning, Sarah awakened from her restless sleep as she felt Tom stirring beside her. She sat up shaking her head groggily as her hand moved automatically to feel the back of his neck. She rose to her knees when her fingers told her of the healthy warmth that had displaced the torrid heat that previously ravaged his body.

She started when she heard him whisper in a weak, scratchy voice, "Sarah . . . Sarah. Do you suppose you could spare a drink of water?"

"Tom," she squealed excitedly. "Tom. Oh, thank God." She squeezed his arm and bent over, planting a warm kiss to his cheek. When she moved to fetch the canteen, Stone Dog had already scaled the escarpment and glided to Tom's side.

Tom was too weak to say more, and the black circles beneath his hollow eyes warned that he was far from out of danger. His hard, trim body had already taken on a sickly, emaciated look, and a cursory examination of the wound disclosed that it was beginning to bulge again from the purulence building up from within. With Sarah's help, Tom took a few swigs from the canteen and swallowed a few crusty bits of roasted rabbit washed down with another mouthful of water. In a few moments, his head bobbed drowsily and flopped against his chest, as his eyes closed in sleep.

Later in the afternoon, he gulped down nearly half the canteen, and some of the filmy glaze had left his eyes. In spite of his improvement, Stone Dog decided they would have to drain the wound again. As the white-hot blade penetrated Tom's raw, tender flesh, he felt like he was reliving the nightmarish moment of his injury, and he dropped off again into senselessness.

When he awoke near sundown, however, he was famished and devoured an ample portion of rabbit with enthusiasm, and a healthier glint replaced the foggy, confused look in his eyes. Now, he was alive to Sarah's presence, and his eyes followed her every move about the ledge.

"Sarah," he rasped, "you look tired. I've put you through quite an ordeal, haven't I?"

She moved beside him and knelt down, taking his hands in hers. He liked the natural impulsive way she always touched him, sometimes pressing his hand and, at others, squeezing his arm or brushing his cheek. There was nothing brazen about it; it was entirely innocent and spontaneous on her part. She was just a toucher.

"You didn't put me through anything, Tom," she chided gently. "The Indians did. . . . And I can't forget you wouldn't be here if I hadn't talked you into it."

"You didn't talk me into anything," Tom protested. "I decided for myself I was coming."

"No," she said. "You thought you made up your own mind, but I decided for you . . . you just didn't know it."

"Well, I'm in no shape to argue with you now."

"You're finally learning something," she teased. She placed her fingers softly on his eyelids and pressed them shut. "And now, you need some more sleep." He did not argue.

Tom was awake that night when Sarah crawled under the blankets and snuggled up against him, her arm curled around his waist. Her nearness kindled his passion, a good sign, he thought. "Sarah," he whispered, "is this what I've been missing the last couple of days?"

"It's a cinch you're feeling better," she said, "but I think it's going to be a long time before you're much danger to anybody."

The warmth of Sarah's body gave Tom a relaxed, comfortable feeling, and, as he drifted off into deep slumber, he thought this could get to be a mighty nice habit.

21

TOM FLINCHED AND gritted his teeth as Sarah pressed the keen knife point into his wound. The pain was excruciating, but he was grateful for the relief that came when he felt the acrid-smelling liquid pour from the wound and drip down his ribs.

"Damn it, Sarah, not so hard," he gasped as she squeezed the flesh around the opening in order to force out the residue of pus and tainted juices.

Ignoring his protests, Sarah observed clinically, "There's not nearly as much as there was a few days ago. We'll probably only have to drain it another week or so. The festering seems to be mostly near the surface now. By the way, in case you're interested, Stone Dog thinks you're going to live. I certainly wouldn't know it by the way you moan and carry on, though."

Tom could not figure this woman out. Up until today, she had been all sympathy and kindness, tending promptly to his every whim. Earlier this morning she had started to seem less attentive, however, insisting firmly, that he feed himself. After breakfast, she and Stone Dog had helped him to his feet for the first time, but he had passed out from the dizzying weakness that swept his legs when the searing pain shot through his shoulder and upper back like a red-hot iron. When he came to, Sarah chastised him properly for giving up so easily and announced that he would be walking tomorrow—or he could fix his own meals. Hell, he couldn't even stand; how did she think he was going to walk?

A good ten days had passed since the lance struck him down, and Tom admitted to himself that he was becoming mildly resentful of his dependence on his companions for his every personal need. A southern gentleman was raised with a certain degree of modesty, and he still was not comfortable about Sarah's supervision of his toilet requirements. As he gradually regained his strength, he was increasingly distressed about the whole situation. Several days ago, he had tactfully suggested to Sarah that Stone Dog might be willing to help with some of his more delicate bodily functions. Sarah had laughed and needled, "Oh, you men, you all think you've got something special in your britches. Well, Stone Dog has more important things to do, and I assure you, I find no pleasure in these little chores. No one will be more delighted than I when you can get off your fanny and take care of yourself."

His musings were cut short when Stone dog climbed up on the ledge and, cocking his Winchester, readied himself behind the barricades. "Somebody comes," he said.

Sarah snatched up Tom's rifle and moved beside the Indian. They watched tensely as the trail of dust spun toward the stronghold like a small cyclone whipping through the prairie grass. Finally, the big, dark man straddled on the bay horse and leading a string of horses came into view.

"It's Joe," Sarah exclaimed, "Joe's back! He made it."

Dropping her rifle, she scrambled down the rocks and dashed like a little girl to the oncoming rider.

No sooner had Joe dismounted than Sarah flew into his arms, hugging him ecstatically, like a child with a big teddy bear, tears of joy streaming from her excited eyes.

"Sarah," Joe said, "what about Tom. Is he—"

"He's going to be all right, Joe. He's grouchy as a hungry grizzly, but he'll be okay. Now that you're here, we can get some decent food in him so he can get his strength back. Go see him. Stone Dog and I can take care of the horses and put away the supplies. Thank God you're back."

22

THE FRESH PUNGENT smell of new-cut pine cleared Tom's
nostrils as the sap bubbled from the logs where the flickering
orange flames were just beginning to take hold. They were
building up a big fire, he knew, for his sake, risking observation
by hostiles in order to fend off the piercing cold that gave him
goose bumps as it crept into his bones. A bitter wind whipped
sharply against the stone escarpment, warning that a long, cold
night was in store for its occupants.

Sarah and the three men gazed silently at the dazzling flames
as they finally commenced to consume the too-green wood and
shoot higher, bouncing the fire's warm glow off the faces of the
entranced observers.

Joe broke the spell. "Well, where do we go from here?" he
asked, poking aimlessly with a stick at the red-hot coals beneath
the flames.

Sarah answered firmly, "Nowhere. Tom won't be able to ride
for days, maybe weeks. We'll stay here till he's fit to ride. We have
water close by and now that you're back, we've got food and
everything else we need. We can stay right here for a long time, if

we have to."

Tom protested, "Just give me a couple of days, and I'll be ready to—"

"Oh, don't be so damned noble," Sarah interrupted. "You can't even stand up by yourself. You're not going to do anybody any good if you fall off your horse out in the middle of God knows-where."

Tom knew he was whipped and pouted quietly as the others planned for the days ahead. It didn't seem like he carried much weight in the camp right now. Evidently, General Kesterson was assuming command.

He liked Sarah's grit. She had iron in her backbone, and he had always been attracted to strong and independent women. But, damn it, ever since he'd been down and out, it seemed like she tried to run the whole show. Well, give him a few more days, and he'd change that.

Finally, Sarah said, "Tom needs to get some sleep, and I think we could all use some rest. Joe, do you suppose you could help me move my bedroll and things off this ledge? Now that Captain Carnes is feeling better, I'll be moving down with Stone Dog." She looked at Tom mischievously. "I'm certain the captain will appreciate your company much more than mine."

"Yes, ma'am," Joe answered, his teeth flashing as he rose to help her.

Tom's irritation turned to puzzlement when Sarah bent spontaneously and kissed him softly on the forehead, as she pulled her bedroll away from his side. "Good night, Tom," she whispered. "Be a good boy."

She slipped away quietly into the night. As Sarah left, Tom suddenly felt very lonely; he could not fathom his reaction, but it was almost like a part of him had climbed down the ledge with her. And to think he was so damned mad at her a few minutes ago.

That night, he slept restlessly, tossing and twisting as his body unconsciously sought the warmth of the one that no longer lay beside him. Joe, stretched out on the other side of the crackling fire, observed Tom's apparent discomfort and draped another blanket over his back, but it offered little relief.

23

TOM PACED BACK and forth in front of the bluff, his eyes casting nervously across the broad valley that lay beyond. It had been nearly a month since Joe's return, and Tom was like a race horse waiting at the startling gate—skittish and impatient to be on the move.

He glanced back at the stark bluff, his eyes moving reflectively to the rustic village that had risen at its base. Two small, thatched, sleeping hutches rested at the foot of the granite escarpment where Sarah and Stone Dog had fashioned temporary homes. A small oven had been improvised from mud and stones by Stone Dog in front of Sarah's small dwelling. Deer and buffalo hides were stretched on long, upright poles scattered randomly about the camp. Now, a sturdy ladder led from the ground level to the rock shelf where Tom and Joe resided. Crusty, stiff deer hides had covered pine beams to form a roof that spanned the ledge and angled down to meet a wall of granite rocks, chinked with shale splinters and mud. It almost looked like some kind of medieval watchtower, Tom thought to himself.

He realized now, that the habitations had sprung up less

from necessity than from the desire of the occupants to keep busy during the long wait. As he slowly regained his strength, even Tom had taken active interest in the construction and assisted to the extent his physical limitations permitted. He had first sat in the saddle again a week ago, and, after he had cantered the horse around the camp a few times, insisted he was ready to go. He started packing his gear in readiness to move out, but Sarah had adamantly refused to travel. He admitted to himself now, that she had been right.

But finally, today, he was ready to ride. Although still bony and gaunt, Tom had recovered some of his lost weight. The color had come back to his face, although his chin and cheeks were an unnatural, chalky white where his rusty beard had been shaved clean a few days previous. He rubbed the foreign smoothness of his jaw and wondered how he'd given in to Sarah's pointed suggestion that he would look less like a mountain goat if he sheared the luxuriant foliage.

As a concession to his gimpy shoulder, he had even allowed Sarah to do the tedious cropping and paring. He had been rewarded amply, however, when after the completion of the job, Sarah had teased, "My, I'd forgotten how handsome and dashing you could look." Then she had smiled and, without warning, planted her moist lips on his soft cheek and scurried away.

He knew, deep down, that the scraggly beard would not take root in his face again. Somehow, Sarah always seemed to get her way with him, and, for some damn reason, he did not really mind —he found himself wanting to please her.

The major remaining physical effect of Tom's brush with death was a restrictive stiffness extending from the top of his right shoulder to the ugly, strawberry-red scar tissue that crinkled into a crevice-like depression below the shoulder blade. When he attempted to raise his right arm above shoulder level, it felt like a drying rawhide strip was looped around his upper arm, pulling the limb downward, as prickly, needlelike darts of pain shot through the scapula above the scar. The joint seemed to loosen and become more pliant daily, but Tom suspected that the severed muscle and tissue would always impose some limitation on his movement.

Well, today, they should be on their way, but they were damn fools to be heading into the Rockies in early November. Winter's icy blast could strike anytime in those mountains, and they'd be in a hell of a fix if they got caught up there in a snowstorm. Miners were already pulling out of the Black Hills in anticipation of an early winter, but anything that would hit here would be nothing compared to the wicked, devastating blizzards that tore unmercifully through the Rockies when winter set in. But they had to chance it. Stone Dog said that most of the Oglala had moved west—evidently to join villages on the Little Big Horn and Little Powder rivers.

Billy's trail was already stone cold. If they didn't find him soon, they could forget about it. If he was alive now, chances were damn slim that he would be after a winter with the Oglala.

Tom walked toward the base of the bluff, where his companions were readying the horses. Sarah greeted him with a mock frown. "Joe just about loaded the pack horses by himself," she said haughtily. "You seemed to be too preoccupied to saddle your own horse, Captain, so I took care of it for you. Seems to me like you've become kind of used to being waited on hand and foot."

He bristled defensively, and softened just as quickly, when

her laughing, sparkling eyes revealed he was being teased again. I've got to quit taking myself so seriously, he admonished himself.

"Thanks, Sarah," he smiled, and then, with a suggestive wink, "I'll do something for you sometime."

Planting a gentle elbow to Tom's ribs, she moved to her own gelding. Mounting, she seemed to be relinquishing command when she said, "I'm ready to go find Billy, Captain."

24

IN A GRANITE-rimmed canyon some five miles northeast of the pursuers, pots and pans clanged noisily as Jasper and Billy struggled to load the uncooperative Lucy. Jasper inched carefully up behind the old "mountain canary," the miners' nickname for the long-eared, obstinate beasts that carried enormous burdens with surefooted aplomb over often-treacherous mountain trails. He reached carefully over the burro's rump to snatch the end of the rope that was to finish the diamond hitch anchoring the load on Lucy's back.

Billy heard a dull thud and then Jasper's anguished moan, as the gangly man stumbled backward and fell to the ground, rubbing his painful shin bone.

"You mangy, old fleabag!" Jasper yelled. "You shoulda been bear food a long time ago."

The old burro's ears lay back flat against her head, narrow slits of eyes glaring out between thick, wrinkled eyelids, daring Jasper to try again. Jasper's face was tomato-red. Billy had never heard him swear, but he was as mad right now as he had ever seen him.

Billy stepped over to the burro, grabbed the rope, pulled it tight, and quickly finished the hitch. There was no reaction from Lucy.

"I think maybe you just got yourself a job," Jasper said. "I've got more bruises than I can count from that cursed critter. Once she laid me up for three days."

"Me and Lucy get along just fine," said Billy. "You just got to talk nice to her, Jasper. . . . Be her friend."

"We'll just have to see about that," said Jasper. "Anyhow, a few more weeks and we'll be in Cheyenne for the winter. Then I'll be rid of her for a while . . . and maybe, you can find your folks."

"My folks are gone," Billy said dejectedly. "You and Crawdad are the only folks I got anymore."

Billy had been at the miners' camp for nearly a month. He had recovered quickly after his discovery by Lucy, and Crawdad and Jasper had informally assumed responsibility for his well-being. Billy more than earned his keep, helping Jasper with the meals and performing other chores around the camp. Crawdad had even lent Billy the utensils for panning gold, and the boy had accumulated his own small stake.

Now the camp was closing and most of the miners were going to Cheyenne for the winter. Ordinarily, they would have worked another few weeks, but Crawdad insisted there was going to be an early winter. The fur on the beaver was longer than switch grass, he pointed out, and the chilling winds that ripped down the canyon at night were coming too early. Some of the men did not want to leave yet. They had heard about a big strike up north at a place called Deadwood Gulch, and those that did not want to stay were itching to move north. In spite of their protests, however, when Crawdad stubbornly began to pack his gear, everybody else followed suit. Although the miners' camp had no formal organization, the unassuming Crawdad wielded great influence among the men and was their unelected leader.

Jasper took Lucy's lead rope and tugged gently. "Good girl, Lucy," he whined with his nasal voice. "You'll come with your old friend, Jasper, won't you . . . won't you?"

The burro jerked her head back and bucked defiantly as Crawdad hobbled up to Billy and wrapped his thick, rough arm around his shoulders. "Well, young feller, looks like them two's still at it. Don't know why, they just never hit it off. Anyhow, I guess we're just about ready to head out of here. You anxious to get going?"

At the query, Billy's blue eyes widened, moisture glazing their surface. "Yes, sir," he answered, "but I'm a little worried."

"There's nothin' to worry about, Billy. I got a lot of friends in Cheyenne. Somehow, we'll find out about your family. Anyways, we're not just goin' to throw you to the wolves. We'll work out something when we get there."

He stepped over and took the cross old burro's lead rope from Jasper and yelled, "I'm headin' for Cheyenne, boys! Anybody wants to come along, you're welcome."

He started up the narrow, winding trail that led out of the camp. Lucy followed obediently; so did Billy and the other miners.

25

THE FOUR RIDERS rode cautiously down the loose, rocky trail that led into the canyon, eventually dismounting and leading the horses as they approached a caved-off section of the path that barely let them by. A single misstep would send man or animal plunging several hundred feet to the chasm floor below.

As they walked out onto the bare, stone flat bordering the swift-running creek that seemed to gouge its way through the canyon bottom, Stone Dog pointed to an old deserted log shack downstream buttressed against the near canyon wall. "Trapper's camp," he said matter-of-factly. "Gone many moons."

Tom surveyed the decaying remnants of the camp. Brave men, he thought—or foolish—to be seeking furs right in the middle of the Sioux lands. The old mountain men were a dying breed and the trapper who had lived here alone, or with a squaw, had likely lost his scalp by now.

If there was such a thing as a good spot in these parts, though, the man had picked it. Trapping should have been good since the canyon appeared to broaden farther upstream where the rock surrendered to grass and aspen groves, no doubt lush with beaver and other fur-bearing creatures. One thing for sure, Indians would have to approach the camp from far to the north or single file down the almost impassable trail they had just travelled. The east and west walls climbed vertically upward for hundreds of feet, certainly impossible to scale, and farther south they narrowed to a bottleneck, through which the creek poured turbulently. The crushing force of the water and the depth of the creek at this point made access from this end of the canyon insurmountable. And yet, escape was possible by entering the same creek and catapulting with the raging water though the exit. Someone had selected the camp shrewdly.

He said to the others, "This looks like a pretty good place for a base camp. We'll stay here for a few days until we decide our next step. Stone Dog says the head of the Little Powder River should be just a few miles northwest. All signs indicate there are at least several major Sioux villages up that way, but we'll have to do some scouting to find where Billy's at." He paused. If he's here at all." Catching a glimpse of Sarah as she bit her lip apprehensively, he wished instantly he had not said the last part. He added quickly, "We haven't come all this way for nothing; we should find Billy in the next couple of days."

They stashed their supplies and bedrolls in the rundown trapper's shack. The glittering quartz canyon wall formed one side of the shack, and stone chips and gravel provided the floor, but it was a roof over their heads and a barrier against the cutting winds that were certain to tear down the canyon come nightfall. The dry, red clay that once secured the stones for the tiny fireplace had crumbled and left the rocks in a heap on the floor. There would be no fire in the cabin this night.

Stone Dog built a small cooking fire outside the shack using only the driest branches in order to make a nearly smokeless blaze. The fire would be extinguished before dark to reduce the chances of discovery by the Sioux.

When they bedded down for the night, as usual, each took a turn as lookout. Sarah took first watch and stood quietly outside the cabin door, her eyes fixed intently on the north end of the canyon. In the early days of their journey, Tom had worried about Sarah's taking a shift at the night watch, uncertain that she could handle it; he knew better now. Sarah gave no quarter, and asked none.

The next morning, Stone Dog and Joe climbed the painstaking trail out of the canyon in search of the Sioux camps. Tom remained behind reluctantly, admitting he could use a day out of the saddle. He still had not recovered his full strength, and his shoulder ached increasingly as the days got colder. He knew he had better be rested and ready when the time came to free Billy.

When the two riders finally disappeared over the canyon rim, Tom scrambled up to the cabin roof and, there, leaning back against the cold canyon wall, cradled his Winchester on upraised knees and turned his eyes toward the far end of the canyon. Sarah busied herself below with the camp chores and hummed softly as she moved in and out of the cabin. Her voice was soothing and seemed to blend in harmony with the singsong rush of the creek waters nearby. Tom watched her out of the corner of his eye and was struck by her grace and femininity in spite of the leather boots and denim trousers she wore. Her hair had grown considerably since the day they left the Double C, and he liked the way the golden locks were now just starting to curl like goosedown over the back of her slender neck.

The bright, midmorning sun finally bounced against the canyon wall radiating a warmth that suited Tom's mood, and he started to feel drowsy, his head bobbing slowly and snapping upright as he jerked himself to his senses. He came alive, however, when he spotted a flash of light apparently reflecting from something metallic up the canyon. It could have been the sun's rays glancing off one of the pieces of quartz or mica that were spread so freely along the chasm bottom. He focused his attention to where he had seen the momentary flicker and waited. Shortly, it flashed again, too much like sun on metal.

"Sarah," he warned, "There may be somebody riding this way. See if you can move the horses farther south, around the bend. Then beat it back here, fast."

Whoever it was would be a good mile away, but another flash of light confirmed that the visitor was coming in their direction. As Sarah returned from moving the horses, Tom clambered off the roof.

"Who is it, Tom?" she asked.

"Can't tell," Tom replied, "but we'd better be ready for trouble. The hell of it is, if we fire our guns, we'll be telling the whole Sioux nation somebody's down here. Anyway, let's get behind the cabin."

As they waited for some further sign of the intruder, Tom peered cautiously around the corner of the cabin, catching movement in the brush along the creek upstream. Abruptly, a young, Sioux buck astride a spotted pony rode into the clearing not more than two hundred yards away, a shiny rifle gripped loosely in his hand, showing Tom the source of the flashing light. He appeared to be alone.

Tom leaned over to Sarah, who stood at his side, back tight

against the cabin wall. "It's a Sioux," he whispered. "Looks like he's coming this way. I could nail him easy enough, but with the echo in this canyon we'd wake up every Indian for miles. Damn . . . of all the luck."

"Tom," Sarah said, "listen . . . what if I let him see me. If he came after me, maybe you could move in from behind and get him without shooting."

"Might work, but it's just too damn risky, Sarah," he responded.

Before he could stop her, Sarah had moved from behind the cabin and was walking nonchalantly southeasterly toward the creek. Angered momentarily, he started after her and then stopped, realizing it was too late, and edged back behind the cabin.

The young Sioux, long black braids hanging over his deerskin shirt, spotted Sarah instantly but did not move. His eyes darted back and forth uneasily and Tom could hear the clicking sound as the buck cocked his rifle. Sarah pretended not to see the young Indian as she approached the creek and bent down, scooping water in her hands as if to drink.

The Indian, sensing the opportunity for surprise, kneed his pony ahead and rode slowly and cautiously downstream toward Sarah. Tom could feel his palms moisten as the Sioux moved closer, the pony's hooves crunching against the broken rocks and shale. He saw Sarah raise her head and look toward the approaching Indian. Feigning surprise, she bolted upright and dashed, as if terror-stricken, farther downstream. The Sioux dug his heels in the pony's flanks and charged recklessly, like a coyote after a jack rabbit.

Tom huddled close to the ground as the pony galloped past

his hiding place and closed in on Sarah. Quickly, he slipped around the corner and entered the cabin, snatching the saber from his bedroll. As he came back out, he saw Sarah suddenly stop and turn to face the Sioux. As the Indian reined in the pony, and slid to the rocky ground, he was met with Sarah's icy glare. The buck set his rifle aside and with a twisted smile, moved toward Sarah, scratching meaningfully at his breechclout. He grabbed her wrist and jerked her toward him as Tom rushed in, his saber pointed lethally.

The buck, picking up the movement behind him, threw Sarah harshly to the ground and leaped for his rifle as Tom bore down. Just as the Sioux pulled the rifle to his shoulder to fire, Tom's saber hacked like a timber axe into the Indian's forearm, slashing well into the bone. The rifle clanked against the shale as it bounced under the Indian's pony, and blood formed pools on the ground as it spewed from his mangled arm. With his good hand, he pulled a keen, narrow-bladed knife from a wrinkled, buckskin sheath hanging at his side, and, with a blood-curdling yell, leaped in the air toward Tom who stumbled backwards, thrusting the sword with a mighty, upward drive, as he fell to the ground. The Sioux fell after him, the sword impaling him through the midsection, its bloody point emerging near his spine. Tom rose, rolling the Sioux away, withdrawing the saber with a single motion.

Sarah grabbed the reins of the Sioux pony and moved to Tom's side. "Tom, are you all right?" she asked worriedly as he rubbed his tightening, aching shoulder.

"Yeah," he said, breathing heavily. "The old shoulder just wasn't ready for this kind of work yet." Then, turning to her, "What was the idea of running out there like that? What if he had just shot instead of chasing after you?"

"But he didn't," she reminded him.

"Well, I'll say this . . . you're one tough lady," he sighed as he walked away to get a shovel. "But if you were in the army, you'd have been shot by now for insubordination."

"You're a pretty tough hombre, yourself, Captain," she called after him. "But I'm not afraid of tough guys," she added.

26

JOE AND STONE Dog did not return that night, but Tom was not especially alarmed. Stone Dog had indicated they might be gone several days, and they would probably not return until they had located the camp where they thought Billy might be.

Tom had doused the fire before dark. He had left the camp momentarily to relieve his bladder and, as he walked back, his eyes scanned the dark, endless space above him. Not a star in the sky tonight, he observed, and with the wind whipping though the canyon, he could tell it was not going to be a very pleasant night.

Suddenly, he was startled by the appearance of a dark form looming in the creek, and he drew his Peacemaker, crouching instinctively in readiness.

"Hi, Tom," the woman's voice called cheerfully. "Come and join me."

Perplexed, he walked toward Sarah's voice. He stopped abruptly in awe and confusion as he came to the edge of the creek and saw Sarah sitting neck-deep, her back resting against a huge boulder, as the icy waters swept around her. The clothes spread out on top of the boulder confirmed his suspicions that she was stark naked.

"Are you crazy?" he said. "That water's ice-cold freezing."

"My dad always said cold water helped the circulation," Sarah answered. "Helps the smell, too. And, with all due respect, I think you're ready for a bath, Captain Carnes," she teased. She giggled mischievously, and her white, rounded breasts bobbed above the surface momentarily.

Tom gulped and felt that familiar stirring in his trousers again. "Yeah, well, have a nice bath, Sarah," and he started walking back to the shack.

"Captain Carnes," Sarah taunted, "you're a coward and you smell like a billy goat. What's the matter . . . you Johnny Rebs afraid of water?"

Ruffled, Tom made an about face and marched toward Sarah. Shaking his finger at her sternly, he said, "Now, listen, Sarah, there's no call to be this way about—"

"Captain Carnes, would you please be gentleman enough to turn around?" Sarah said disdainfully, as she stood up in the creek. "I swear, you southern gentlemen have no sense of propriety whatever."

Tom turned quickly, catching an ample glimpse of her well-proportioned body in spite of the dark. As she dressed, he could hear the rustling of her clothes, and the images he conjured in his mind nearly drove him wild.

Shortly, Sarah said, slightly more condescending, but still with a tone of mockery, "Good night, Tom. You really do need to take a bath.

He stood there dumbfounded as he watched her walk away. "Oh, what the hell," he muttered to himself, and he started pulling off his boots. Stripping to the buff, Tom leaped to Sarah's spot in the creek and, slipping on the slick, grease like stones, tumbled backward into the creek. "Jesus Christ!" he screamed as the frigid water swirled around his neck. He shot from the creek like a cat that had its tail stepped on. Shivering uncontrollably and teeth chattering, he pulled on his trousers and, snatching up his other clothes, dashed for the camp.

Sarah was waiting with a blanket to wrap around him. "Oh, you look ever so much healthier, Captain Carnes. Smell better, too, I must say. By the way, they also tell me that a cold bath does wonders for inflamed passions. Is that right, Captain?" she said with mock naivety.

Tom just looked at her in disgusted silence, but his cold, shriveled organ answered in the affirmative.

Later, as Tom curled up his thick bedroll, his shoulder throbbing with dull pain, he felt the damp coldness crawling down from the mountains. It will frost tonight, he thought, and that damn wind won't help anything. He shivered and pulled the blankets over his ears. Then he heard Sarah scooting into her own blankets next to his. Still smarting from her earlier needling, he feigned sleep. He felt Sarah's hand touch his shoulder gingerly.

"Tom," she asked with genuine concern, "your shoulder hurts, doesn't it?"

"Just a little," he responded guardedly.

"Can I rub it for you?" she said, and without waiting for a response, pulled the blanket from his shoulder and began kneading and massaging his back and tender shoulder gently. After a time, his eyelids became heavy, and, as he dropped off to sleep, his last memory was of Sarah snuggling up behind him, emanating a warmth reminiscent of the fireplace at Red Oaks plantation.

27

LATE THE FOLLOWING afternoon, Joe and Stone Dog rode into camp. The Indian's face was impassive and told Tom nothing. As Joe dismounted, however, Tom read trouble in the firm set of his jaw and the grim tightness of his mouth.

"Well, spill it out," Tom said, as he took the two horses.

Joe said, "We're almost positive we found the right Sioux village. Stone Dog says it's an Oglala camp . . . likely Crazy Horse's bunch." Joe went on to explain that he and Stone Dog had observed the village for most of the previous afternoon and then scouted its perimeters early this same morning. They saw no sign of Billy, but they did see a huge, black-bearded man who matched Sarah's description of Bear.

Stone Dog sketched a rough map in the dust as Joe elaborated. The Oglala village was located near one end of an expansive, grassy, spring-fed valley not far from the Little Powder River. One side of the village ended at the base of the same ridge of barren buttes that ultimately led southward to form one flank of the canyon where they were now camped. The other three sides had no natural barriers and blended into lush, open meadows that did not give way to the surrounding mountains for some miles. Protected by the mountains and with bountiful forage for their ponies, the Sioux had probably established a permanent village there, Joe noted.

"You can't ride near the camp from the meadows without being spotted," Joe said. "Stone Dog and I agree that the only way we can get into camp is down the slopes behind. They're steep enough in a few places, but otherwise, they drop off fairly gradual. Anyhow, we want you to hear us out on the plan we've come up with."

Joe pointed out that the slope leading to the camp was impassable for a horse, but it could be scaled without great difficulty by a man. It would be easier to get into the village than to get out, since the exit up the incline would be slow and tedious, exposing the climbers to considerable danger if discovered. Once reaching the mountain crest there were two possible escape routes. One was over a series of trails that branched southwesterly leading ultimately to Fort Fetterman over one hundred miles to the south. The other was southeasterly in the direction of the canyon where they were now camped. There was no town or army outpost for miles, but Fetterman could eventually be reached over this route by making a wide circle eastward to the edge of the Black Hills and then traveling southwest again.

"Here's what we think we ought to do," said Joe. "Stone Dog and I should climb down into the village and—"anticipating Tom's protest—"if we have to help a little boy out of there, Tom, your gimpy shoulder might keep us from having the edge we need. If you'll think like a soldier, you'll know I'm right." He continued, "We'll find this man called Bear and, one way or the other, we'll find out if Billy's in camp—" he hesitated and glanced uncomfortably toward Sarah—"or what's happened to him. If the boy's in the village, we'll find him and beat it out of there. Tom, we'll have you and Sarah posted on the hillside to provide us cover if we need it."

"After we get to the top, we'll split up. Stone Dog and I will take the southwest trail toward Fetterman. We'll leave signs for the Sioux to follow, and, since it's the most likely escape route, they'll be more apt to go that way. Tom, you can take Sarah and the boy and head back this way—we'll leave the pack horses and supplies here—stay in the canyon a few days, and then take the long way out. We'll rendezvous at Fetterman; Stone Dog will tell you how to get there before we leave. Even if the Sioux don't swallow the whole bait, we're bound to confuse them and buy more time. Anyhow, Stone Dog says, with winter coming on, the Sioux aren't so interested in making war, and we're likely only to have a few of the more ambitious bucks on our trail. Well, what do you think?"

Sarah said, "I don't know. I'd like to know what Tom has to say about it."

Tom was thoughtfully silent. "There isn't a good plan for this situation," Tom said, "but I think you're right—this is the best we can come up with. I've been to Fetterman and know the country around there pretty well. If Stone Dog can steer me in the right direction, we should be able to make it. When do we go?"

"We figured early afternoon tomorrow," answered Joe. "We can be there in three hours.

"We want to get there before dark so we can try to spot this Bear character, but we won't want to go into the camp until after dark. The Sioux are nervous about traveling at night, and old Stony says they won't look too hard till morning."

"Let's hope they don't look too hard any time," said Tom.

28

BILLY PULLED THE warm goosedown quilt over his ears and pressed his head into the soft, fluffy pillows as he curled up on the straw-filled mattress beneath him. A streak of light crept beneath the door, and he heard the boisterous laughter of men and women ringing from the rooms down the hall. He closed his eyes and fell quickly to sleep, secure in the assurance that he was once again among his own kind.

Crawdad and Jasper had deposited Billy at the Grate mansion when they had ridden, tired and saddle sore, into Cheyenne late that afternoon. The two men had spent a good part of the day arguing about Billy's disposition.

"A whorehouse ain't a fit place for a boy," Jasper had insisted.

"Oh, hell," Crawdad had countered, "This boy needs a woman's touch real bad. He lost his mama, and he ain't been with nobody but savages and a bunch of gold-crazy miners for weeks. Yep, he needs a woman bad. . . . In a different way, maybe, than you and me . . . but just the same, he needs a woman. Besides, can you name a better person in the whole world than Big Wilma?"

Jasper could not.

When they rode up in front of the big, white house, Billy's eyes widened in awe. He had never seen such place—two stories high and an honest-to-goodness covered porch with rocking chairs and benches. As they stepped on the porch, Big Wilma paraded out of the door and grabbed Crawdad with a big bear hug, lifting him a good foot in the air. Kissing the old man lavishly on the lips and cheeks, she laughed raucously.

"Crawdad, you old fart, I thought you'd never get back to see Big Wilma," and then, seeing Billy, "Oh, sorry, honey. Crawdad, who's your handsome young friend?"

Crawdad told how he had found Billy at the miners' camp. When he related what had happened to Billy's mother and family, huge tears rolled down Wilma's fat jowls, and she pulled the boy to her gargantuan bosom.

"He'll stay here with me till he decides what he wants to do . . . and don't you dare say otherwise, you dirty old . . . man. Now Billy, honey, you just come in here with me," she said as she led the boy through the door. She turned back to the old miner. "Crawdad, you've got yourself a special reservation with Big Wilma tonight. After you get that mud scraped off, you just come up and we'll . . . talk awhile. Okay?" she winked.

The grizzled miner's face turned a bright scarlet; Jasper coughed nervously.

At supper that evening, Billy had almost foundered himself on fried chicken and mashed potatoes, finished off with two big pieces of apple pie. A gracious hostess, Big Wilma, a silver-haired lady in her mid-fifties, weighed nearly two hundred pounds, was a sharp contrast to the sleek, voluptuous ladies that joined them at the table. Billy had never seen so many pretty ladies gathered in one place, and he was especially smitten by Carmella, an olive-skinned woman with round, black eyes, who laughed a lot, and made a big fuss over him. Even at his young age, he was entranced by the cleavage between the bulges that looked like they were about to pop out of her low-cut gown. The young creole woman had a smooth, soft voice. Strangely, she had a way with words, and when she spoke in her barely perceptible French accent, it was like warm honey rolling off her lips. Billy gazed at the young woman dreamily; he did not know what a whorehouse was, but he thought it was a nice place to be.

After breakfast the next morning, Crawdad came to visit Billy and Big Wilma. They sat at the table in the warm cozy kitchen, Crawdad fingering a tin cup of black, steaming coffee nervously.

"Come on, old man, out with it. You weren't so slow on the draw last night," Big Wilma laughed, jabbing an elbow sharply to his ribs.

Wiping coffee from his whiskers, Crawdad said, "I checked with the sheriff this morning and got some word about Billy's family. Seems like his new deputy was mustered out of the infantry at Camp Robinson in Nebraska a few weeks back. Billy's sister had been there not many weeks before."

Billy's face brightened, and he grinned broadly. "I knew it, I knew it," he said excitedly.

"The deputy," said Crawdad, "told me that Billy's folks had been killed by a Sioux raiding party. I guess Billy'd already figured that out, but he never was sure about his sister. Anyhow, she was up at Camp Robinson looking for Billy. The deputy said she was travelin' with the strangest bunch you'd ever seen—some ex-army officer, a big negro, and a dried-up, old Pawnee Indian.

The army must have had some trouble with the men 'cause the deputy didn't speak too highly of them. Anyways, they pulled out. Billy's sister said they was headed for the Black Hills to find her brother. Damn it, they was riding direct into a hornet's nest, and we could've just missed them. Now what do we do with this spunky young feller?" he asked, reaching his hand across the table, mussing Billy's hair affectionately.

"I'll wait here for Sarah," Billy said confidently.

Crawdad said solemnly, "Billy, we don't even know for sure she's still alive. You know as well as I do that the Black Hills is no place to be these days. They could've turned around and gone back home, though we'll notify the authorities down there, and let them know you're here."

"That's okay by me, Crawdad," Billy said, "but you're wasting your time. Sooner or later, Sarah's going to show up here. She'll find me. . . . I know she will. She's a Kesterson just like me."

"I'll bet he's right," chuckled Wilma. "He'll stay with me till his sister shows up."

29

THE FOUR RIDERS slowed their horses to a walk as they rode single file along the crest of the ridge. They traveled light, the pack horses and other supplies having been left at the camp.

With luck, Tom thought, he, Sarah, and little Billy would be back at the cabin by dawn tomorrow. They would hole up there for a few days until the Sioux had a chance to calm down; then they would head for Fort Fetterman to rendezvous with Joe and Stone Dog.

The footing became increasingly uncertain as the firm trail that sloped steeply off one side fragmented and turned to loose shale and fine-grained stone. Tom tugged the fleece-lined collar of his mackinaw up around his neck and pulled his head turtle-like into the depths of the coat.

Searching the overcast sky worriedly, he commented to Sarah who rode behind him, "It's got to be near freezing, and that wind could be nasty before the day's out. I heard Stone Dog tell Joe we could be in for some snow. He said it might be a good thing since the Sioux wouldn't be looking for trouble."

Tom could understand Stone Dog's thinking. If the Oglala

thought it was going to snow, they would be less likely to have scouts on the trail, and that certainly lessened the chances of encountering a stray war party. On the other hand, he did not much like the idea of being caught in these mountains in the middle of a snowstorm, but was likely too early for much of a snow anyway.

The rescuers rode for several hours, halting from time to time while they waited for Stone Dog to scout the trail ahead. Finally, the Pawnee admonished the riders to dismount and lead their horses. Joe noted that they should be only about an hour from the village.

Later, as they came over a rise, Tom could see streams of billowy smoke floating upward from the Sioux village at the base of the mountain below. Through the scattered pine jutting from the steep slopes, he could make out the hide-covered tepees scattered about the village.

Following Stone Dog's lead, they tied their horses in a small ravine that sliced the incline opposite the village.

"There must be fifty tepees in the camp," worried Tom. "It's going to be a job finding the white man, let alone the boy. It's going to get dark early tonight; do you suppose it'd be safe to move down closer now?"

Stone Dog nodded affirmatively and led the group over the crest. They moved snaillike down the treacherous slope, picking their way carefully to avoid sliding on the loose shale that covered much of the surface. Although there were no abrupt drop offs or sheer cliffs, an untimely misstep could send a person sliding and rolling down the mountainside right into the heart of the Oglala camp. The greater risk was the possibility of starting a small rock slide that would most certainly alert the camp to the invasion.

About a third of the way down, Stone Dog gestured for Sarah to pull off and position herself behind a craggy boulder that protruded like a giant tooth from the slope.

"Sarah," Tom said, "we don't want the Sioux to know for sure how many of us are here, so don't shoot unless you absolutely have to. If for some reason, the rest of us don't make it this far, you get the hell out of here and head back to the canyon; then make the circle around to Fort Fetterman the way Stone Dog explained."

Sarah paled noticeably, shadows of concern crossing her eyes. The possibility of failure had not even occurred to her till now, Tom realized.

As he moved to follow Joe and Stone Dog down the incline, Sarah grasped his hand and held him back momentarily. She looked full into his eyes. "Take care," she said softly, releasing his hand reluctantly.

"You, too," he answered.

About halfway down the slope, the men paused at a cluster of scrub pine. "We wait here," said Stone Dog.

Tom glanced back up the mountain and saw Sarah crouched behind the boulder, the dead Indian's Winchester cradled across her forearm. She waved, looking more confident now, and Tom waved back.

They had a clear view of the Sioux village from this point, and the men, sheltered by the green pine needles, studied the camp for the better part of an hour trying to pick up some sign of the boy.

"Getting ready for storm," Stone Dog observed as the camp buzzed with activity.

The squaws rushed about pulling curing hides from the long pole stretchers that dotted the camp. Several of the bucks stitched frantically at the outer walls of their tepees, apparently repairing and replacing the hides that made up the stiff covering. Others gathered ponies, leading them far out into the meadow, evidently to some sanctuary that offered protection from the storm. A brisk wind flapped the buckskin covers that were the tepee doors and, as the gusts increased in strength, an atmosphere of urgency obviously consumed the camp.

Then they saw Bear. The black-maned giant strutted through the camp scratching his bulging paunch like a flea-bitten dog. Tom froze momentarily when the big man stopped suddenly and looked up toward the clump of trees behind which they were hidden and, for a moment, he was certain they had been spotted. He breathed a sigh of relief when the man stomped over to a nearby fire and hunkered down to warm his hands.

Rotating, billowy clouds filled the snow now, and as early darkness descended upon the village, Bear rose and lumbered stiffly to one of the tepees, where a fat, stumpy squaw stacked broken pine branches for firewood. He stooped and crawled into the tepee and was followed soon after by the squaw. Shortly, thick, gray smoke rose from the cone-shaped lodge, evidence that the occupants were settling in for the night.

With the darkness, the cold became numbing, and now Tom could hear the faint, almost animal-like, howl of the wind moving through the valley. He knew that Stone Dog had been right—he could feel the icy dampness in the air that foretold snow, and the gnawing pain in his shoulder confirmed a change in the weather.

"We're going to have to move fast," he whispered to Joe.

"Thank God his tepee's at this end of the camp."

Joe nodded in silent agreement, his obsidian eyes concentrating vulture-like on Bear's lodge.

For the first time, Tom understood why the Pawnee were in such awe of the Black Buffalo. This side of Joe was capable of dealing cold, ruthless death.

The village was silent now except for the occasional barking of a few dogs and the sporadic cries of infants erupting from several of the tepees. "Now," said Stone Dog as he and Joe started down the slope, moving like two stalking cougars toward Bear's tepee.

It rankled Tom's pride to watch his comrades inch their way down the hillside toward the village, leaving him behind. The mood passed quickly, however, as he reminded himself that their job was to get Billy, and that Joe and Stone Dog were best equipped to handle this part of their mission. He glanced back up the mountainside toward Sarah. He could just make out the shadowy outline of her form now, but he knew she was watching; he could count on her, and it gave him confidence.

Joe and Stone Dog dropped to the ground as they drew near the encampment, slithering like two snakes to the back of Bear's lodge. It was one of two tepees set back and off to one side in a corner of the village. There was no sound in the other, and pulling his eyelids closed, Stone Dog signaled that the occupants were asleep. Soft giggling intermingled with heavy, labored grunting came from Bear's tepee as Stone Dog touched his ear to the tight, rawhide covering. His lips parted in a devilish smile and, rolling his single eye, he pointed to his crotch, nodding his head knowingly. Joe smiled back in understanding.

Instantly, Stone Dog's curved-bladed scalping knife appeared in his hand, and with a single sweep, the sliced hides quietly parted. The Pawnee slipped quickly and easily through the narrow opening and Joe followed, though less gracefully, right behind.

Bear, his leathery, white buttocks exposed to the air, was astride the naked, dumpy squaw, and never knew what hit him as the bone handle of Stone Dog's knife thumped him sharply behind the ear, yanking him rudely from the throes of conjugal bliss, rolling limply from the low-set cot to the dirt floor.

Before the squaw could scream, Stone Dog grabbed her chin and, wrenching her head backwards, slid the keen knife blade across her throat. A wheezing, gurgling sound rose from the squaw's throat when he released her head, blood rolling down her chest and dripping from her pendulous breasts as he pushed her to the lodge floor. A stifling odor consumed the tepee as the squaw relieved her bowels in death.

Joe, who had joined Stone Dog, seeing that Bear had rolled in the hot coals of the lodge fire, dragged the big man off to one side, beating and brushing Bear's back to smother the fire smoldering in his buckskin shirt. Momentarily, Stone Dog moved to his side and promptly produced a handful of long rawhide strips and commenced to lash the ends to Bear's wrists and ankles, anchoring the thongs to the sturdy lodge poles. In a few moments, Bear was spread eagled on the floor of the tepee, still naked from the waist down.

The lodge was hot and steamy now. Joe rubbed the sweat from his eyes. He glanced coldly and unfeelingly at the grotesque body of the squaw, lying in a rounded heap on the other side of the tepee. "Now, what?" he whispered.

Stone Dog, his face emotionless, slipped up to Bear's head

and began slapping him lightly, but sharply, on his puffy cheeks. The big man's eyes blinked open. Stone Dog waved his bloody knife in front of Bear's eyes and ran his finger meaningfully along his own lips to convey the unmistakable message of silence.

Bear's eyes rolled to the ghastly form of the squaw, and his expression switched instantly from belligerence to fear.

Joe broke the silence. "Okay, mister, we want some answers, and we want them quick. We came to get a little boy, Billy Kesterson—blond, blue eyes—and don't bother to deny anything. We know you and your friends took him—his sister told us."

At first, Bear looked puzzled, uncomprehending. Then, anger flamed in his eyes. "That Goddamned, yellow-haired bitch," he spat out.

Stone Dog's hand thrust against Bear's mouth, squeezing his jaws together with viselike force, and his knife slashed downward, opening a gaping, sagging gash the length of his cheek. Thick, red blood ran down the side of the big man's face, soaking his matted beard and hair. Stone Dog released the man's lips, again exhibiting the knife menacingly.

"I never touched the boy," he lied, gasping for breath. "Lone Badger—the next tepee—he took the boy for his . . . uh, squaw. He's a strange devil. He likes boys . . . know what I mean? I didn't mean the kid no harm."

"Where is he?" Joe repeated.

"He ain't here, I swear," answered Bear. "He got away just a few days after we got to the hills. Jumped in a creek and washed down the mountain—gotta be dead. No way he coulda lived in them fuckin' mountains." Then, eyeing the Pawnee, "Goddamn, you gotta believe me," he choked.

"What do you think?" asked Joe, his eyes meeting Stone

Dog's.

Stone Dog moved away from Bear's face and knelt near the man's hips. He moved the knife blade slowly toward the vulnerable mass between Bear's legs, studying the man's eyes as the point of his knife pricked his genitals, drawing a few droplets of blood. Goose bumps spread over Bear's body and salty sweat mixed freely with the blood on his face.

"God have mercy," Bear whispered. "I told you the truth." He looked at Joe pleadingly. "Goddamn, mister! Call him off. I told the truth—I swear it, I swear it."

Joe said matter-of-factly, "There aren't many men that would lie with a knife pointing at their balls."

Stone Dog pulled the knife back. "He speaks the truth. Boy's not here," he said.

Joe clenched his fist in frustration and struck it hard against his thigh. "Damn, all this way for nothing, and in a few minutes, we could have half the Sioux nation on our backs. Let's get the hell out of here."

The flap lifted at the tepee opening, and the two men jumped up simultaneously as the icy wind whipped in. There they met the startled face of Lone Badger who let out a bloodcurdling yell that echoed eerily through the village, just before Stone Dog's knife plunged hilt-deep into his chest.

The Indian stared at Stone Dog disbelievingly for a moment and sank to the ground, grasping the rawhide flap and tearing it loose as he fell face down in the dirt.

Joe and Stone Dog darted out the opening in back of the tepee and started up the slope as pandemonium broke loose in the Sioux camp. They could hear Bear's outrageous bellowing rising above the din as they scrambled up the shale and rock.

"Damn it, we should've cut the bastard's throat," Joe said disgustedly.

The going was slow, and they slipped repeatedly on the loose shale, sometimes losing more ground than they gained. Joe glanced over his shoulder and saw Bear pulling on his trousers and barking orders to the warriors who had gathered about his lodge. Bear and a half dozen of the Sioux broke off from the assemblage and charged up the incline in fierce pursuit. Several rifles exploded, and bullets splintered the rocks at Joe's feet.

Then Tom's Winchester cracked steadily, raining bullets on the Sioux. Abruptly, his rifle fire quieted as he stopped to reload. "This way, Joe," Tom yelled. "Hurry up, they're closin' the gap!"

Another rifle cracked from below and Stone Dog faltered, took a few more steps and stumbled to the ground. When he saw the Pawnee's plight, Joe stopped and skidded back to the wounded Indian. Tears glistened in his dark eyes, as he felt the warm, sticky liquid pumping from Stone Dog's back. Gently, he turned him over and read death in the glazed, lone eye.

"No good," Stone Dog gasped. "The great spirit calls. Go to the golden one—run." He implored again, "Run." And then, summoning some hidden reserve of strength, the Pawnee rose, snatching up his rifle, and staggered down the slope, charging directly into the path of his Sioux enemy. His rifle fired three times, dropping two of the stunned Sioux warriors. The singsong wailing of the Pawnee death cry was cut short as Oglala bullets shredded Stone Dog's body, and the old Indian rolled with the sliding shale down the slope.

Seeing there was nothing he could do for the Pawnee comrade, Joe leveled a few quick shots at the Sioux and, as they ducked for cover, continued his retreat up the mountainside.

Instantly, Bear and three or four Sioux warriors were up, chasing after him, their fury mounting as Tom's bullets sprayed the rock in front of them. As he reached the pines where Tom was hidden, Joe dived into the trees, catching his breath, while Tom emptied his Winchester at the pursuers who were now huddled belly-flat against the slope.

"Where's the boy?" Tom asked.

"He's not there," Joe said. "He got away when they reached the Black Hills. Probably dead."

Tom nodded soberly, his eyes continuously searching the slope. He saw more Sioux stirring at the bottom. They could not keep the whole tribe at bay, and that is what they would be facing pretty quick. "You ready?" Tom asked.

"Yeah."

"Let's go," he said, and led the way to the top.

Bullets showered around the two men until Sarah's unrelenting fire slowed the pursuit. Nevertheless, by the time they reached Sarah, Bear and the Indians had closed to within fifty feet, and Joe and Tom slipped in behind the rock to return their fire.

"Tom," Sarah said, "Billy ... where is—"

"He got away awhile back, Sarah," Tom interrupted. "We don't know where he is right now." He decided the rest of the story could wait.

"Stone Dog?" she asked.

"He's dead," Tom replied softly. He squeezed the Winchester trigger as one of the Sioux raised up to leap forward. With almost sadistic pleasure, he heard the Indian yelp and saw him tumble backward down the slope.

In another five minutes, Bear and the remaining two Indians

would be joined by another dozen Sioux, Tom observed.

"Come on," he said, "let's get over the top."

As they inched their way upward, they paused intermittently to return the pursuers' fire. As they reached the top, they had to throw their rifles over the ridge, using their hands to pull themselves up. Sarah went first, Tom giving her a boost as Joe poured a steady stream of lead down the incline. As soon as Sarah climbed over the rim, Tom threw his rifle over and clambered after her. With Tom half suspended on the ledge, Joe's rifle clicked a hollow, empty sound. As he bent to reload, Bear and the two Indians seized upon the moment and charged recklessly up the slope. Bear closed in on Joe aiming his rifle at the mulatto's chest.

"Now, you black bastard—" he roared.

A rifle exploded. Bear's own weapon clanked as it bounced down the slope, and the big man slid and tumbled after it, blood gushing from the hole in his neck, until his unfeeling body came to rest against a lone pine.

Sarah's rifle barked again as Tom pulled himself over the top, and one of the Sioux grabbed his belly and fell to the ground. The other Indian dived for cover, content to wait for the reinforcements moving more cautiously up the slope.

As Joe came over the top he said, "Well, Sarah took care of the big bastard. He's done the last of his killing. Damn, I don't know why we didn't finish him off in the camp."

Tom said, "It doesn't matter now. The main thing is to get the hell out of here—quick. There's no need to split up anymore. Let's head back to the canyon."

The three stopped long enough to spray the mountainside with bullets. Then Tom, noting that the Sioux were losing interest, said, "I don't think they're in a hurry right now. Let's ride."

After they had raced back to the horses and mounted, Tom took the lead heading back the way they had come. Glancing back, he noticed Joe wasn't with them; then saw the mulatto farther back, reining his mount to the southwest. "Joe, hurry up," he said.

"I'll see you at Fetterman, partner." The black man waved and kneed his horse down the other trail.

Tom pulled his horse around to follow, and stopped, as he saw an Indian pull himself over the rim. Tom raised his rifle, aimed deliberately, and squeezed the trigger, and the Sioux toppled backward down the mountainside. Another scrambled over, and Tom called to Sarah, "We're cut off from Joe; we'll have to ride to the canyon."

Without horses, the Sioux could not keep the pace with the riders, and they were safe for the moment. It would be several hours before the Sioux could descend to their camp, round up ponies, and follow, Tom figured. Then there was the question whether they would follow Joe's trail or the route back to the canyon.

As the bitter wind laced his cheeks sharply, Tom's mind turned quickly to other dangers. It occurred to him that with the increasing likelihood of a storm, the Sioux might not even follow, but he knew from his past experience in the Wyoming mountains that a snowstorm could be every bit as much a threat to their lives as the Indians. Anyway, they were temporarily safe from the Sioux.

30

WITHOUT EVEN STARLIGHT to illuminate the trail, Tom and Sarah slowed the horses to a walk as they picked their way across the mountain ridge. Neither had spoken since their separation from Joe.

Finally, Tom broke the awkward silence. "I'm sorry, Sarah. . . . I'm really sorry," he said, as he sidled his horse next to hers and reached across to give her back a gentle pat.

She turned her head toward his and nodded with her quivering lips forming a forced smile, silent tears streaming slowly down her cold, chapped cheeks. "I know," she answered sincerely.

The force of the wind grew to almost hurricane-like proportions and, as they turned to head down the narrow canyon trail, tiny snowflakes began to dot the steel-gray sky. Moving down the trail, Tom saw quickly that it would be suicide to ride the horses down the steep grade this night.

"Sarah," he said, "we'll have to dismount. It's going to take us some time to get down there, but there's no turning back now. Just hug the wall and follow me. If your horse should start to go off, just let him go. Understand?" She did not answer. "Sarah, did you hear what I said?" he asked sternly. He knew they were in trouble and, instinctively, he was a soldier again.

After a long pause, Sarah replied, "I understand."

An hour later, they were still only halfway down the trail which now had become icy and treacherous. Several times, violent blasts of wind slammed against the canyon walls, almost blowing horses and riders off the trail, sending them crashing to the rocks below. Now the snowfall was heavier and beginning to pile up on the path, making it increasingly difficult to tell where the rock wall of the canyon ended and the snow-covered trail began.

Tom stopped for a moment and looked back. Sarah looked done in; her face was flushed, obviously burned raw by the cutting wind that lashed her cheeks. Tom brushed away the frosty ice that had formed in the corners of his eyes. Damn, he was not doing so well himself. They could both freeze to death up here.

"Sarah!" he yelled, pulling his coat up around his ears. "I can't make out the trail anymore. Be sure to stay next to the wall. Hug it just as close as you can. . . . Are you okay?"

"I'll be all right," she answered uncertainly.

"Try to follow my tracks," Tom called. "This is going to be a granddaddy blizzard before the night's out."

They trudged on, painstakingly, down the slippery trail as the wind howled like a banshee through the canyon. Suddenly, behind him, Tom heard the frantic whinnying of the black gelding and clashing of hoof against rock. Turning, he saw Sarah struggling to hold the animal and at the same time, maintain her own delicate balance as the horse slid closer to the trail's edge.

"Let go!" he yelled. Sarah still pulled at the reins. In a second, the horse was going to pull her over. "Sarah! Let go, now!"

She let loose of the reins just as the gelding toppled over the edge, its hideous shrieking sending shivers down Tom's spine until it ended with a sickening thud as the horse hit the canyon floor below. Sarah pressed her back tight against the canyon wall, shocked and petrified, declining to take one step farther down the trail.

"Sarah, come on!" Tom yelled, his voice muffled by the wind. "We've got to keep moving."

She just gazed downward into the seemingly bottomless abyss, shaking her head back and forth, uncomprehending. Finally, slowly and carefully, Tom squeezed between his own horse and the chasm wall and inched his way back toward Sarah.

When he reached her, he took her stiff, frozen hand in his and pulled her to him, cradling her head against his shoulder, his lips brushing her forehead softly. As the bleak wind whipped between their faces, he whispered, "Sarah, I love you. Don't give up on me now." He felt her hands tighten around his back, holding him close as if she were afraid he might somehow escape.

After a few moments, she tilted her head upward slightly and shook her head. "I'm coming." Sanity crept back into her eyes. Hand in hand, they edged by the horse and continued down the trail, each drawing strength from the other. In a short while, the trail began to widen again, telling Tom they were nearing the canyon floor. Still, he did not breathe easily until they reached the trail's end and stepped off onto the solid ground below. He boosted Sarah on the horse and led the mount through the deepening snow toward the rundown trapper's shack.

31

JOE STAYED WITH the high country as he galloped southward. The slicing wind left him numb with cold, but it was a fast trail —plenty of elbow room and few obstructions. He had been traveling the better part of the night, and, as he glanced warily back over his shoulder, he could see no sign of pursuit. He had good reason to feel safe now; some miles up the trail, the white, craggy slopes that framed the Sioux village shone fluorescent-like in the early morning darkness telling him that heavy snow had visited the mountain hideaway.

Until now, Joe had left the snow behind him, and the white flakes could not have come at a better time to cover his escape. The last hour, however, fluffy, scattered snowflakes had started to drift in with the bleak wind and now commenced to gather on the trail forming milky webs on the rocks. As the coal-black sky turned slate gray, the snow worsened, finally obliterating any trails, and Joe reined in his tired, huffing gelding. Off to his left, he sighted a cluster of large boulders to offer sanctuary from the storm. He tied the horse behind the rocks and after unsaddling the animal, snuggled in between the boulders. He built a small fire; then, wrapping himself mummy-like in his blankets, fell quickly to sleep.

He huddled in the rocky haven until mid afternoon that day when the snow gradually faded away and the wind exhausted its fury. A serene quiet came to the low-set mountains, and Joe looked out on a blanket of white. He downed some hardtack and twisted beef jerky, saddled his horse and continued southward along the snowy ridge. Below, he could see a deep, almost unfathomable, sea of oyster-white waves filling the ravines and canyons. In marked contrast, the ridge which he now rode had been swept broom-clean by the raging wind and for the time being, the snow was no obstacle to his progress.

Later, the trail grew more rugged, and the ridge turned spiny, dipping sharply and frequently as Joe turned the horse down the trail toward the open plateaus that promised a speedy journey to Fort Fetterman. Edging the horse down the steep, treacherous incline, Joe found himself increasingly bogged down in the snow that filled the holes and clefts, and his mighty arms strained to their limits as he coaxed and pulled his reluctant mount through one drift after another.

On one such effort, Joe pulled strenuously at the horse's reins, and when the animal lunged forward, his right front foot slipped on the icy stone and turned under, sending him tumbling backward into the drift. When Joe tried to pull the horse free again, he noted that the animal's leg turned at a peculiar angle. Then, kneeling beside the horse, he saw the splintered bone poking through the hide. He untied his bedroll and saddlebags and pulled his Winchester from its scabbard and, patting the horse gently on its neck, he stepped back and slammed the bullet between the animal's eyes. He turned, his face grim, his jaw set firm, and headed down the trail to the flatter lands below.

32

FORT FETTERMAN WAS situated on the south bank of the North Platte River at the mouth of LaPrele Creek, and its low, white buildings perched atop a high, stark bluff made the army outpost visible for some miles. Joe had scouted Fetterman country several years before, and the red clay and sandstone that peeked through the windswept snow told him that the end of his long trek was in sight.

Now the terrain was crisscrossed with ravines and gullies, and Joe scanned the horizon for some familiar sign. He paused, fixing on a long bluff perhaps five miles to the east. He took a deep breath and quickened his pace, trotting for a while, and then slowing to a brisk walk, as he headed for the bluff.

It was turning colder, and the sun was shooting forth its last feeble rays of the day when Joe walked seemingly out of nowhere into the fort. The guards looked on in puzzlement and confusion at the black giant until someone finally summoned the officer of the day.

Abruptly, Joe was confronted by a curious young second lieutenant. "Where in the blazes did you come from, mister?" the

Ron Schwab

lieutenant asked. His manner was friendly.

"Little Powder River country," Joe answered. "I've been walking the better part of two weeks. I'm supposed to meet two friends here—a man and a young woman. They should've made it by now."

"You're the first fellow outside of army that's been here for weeks," the lieutenant said. "They haven't made it yet. You say you've been walking out there two weeks, mister? Christ, you should've been dead days ago. You don't look like you've even missed dinner."

"Well, I've missed a lot of dinners these last days, and I could sure stand something to eat. Then I could sleep for a week." His face turned sober and worry creased his eyes. Joe muttered to himself, "They must be stuck in that damn canyon. I shouldn't have left them."

"What's that, mister?" the lieutenant asked.

"Nothing, lieutenant," Joe said, "just talking to myself. Too many days in the snow, I guess. How about something to eat? If it's all right with you people, I'll stick around this place for a little while. There's not a damn thing I can do for my friends now. If they don't show up in a few days, I'll head down Cheyenne way before winter really takes hold. With all due respect, I sure as hell don't want to spend the next four months here at Fetterman."

"Can't say as I blame you," the lieutenant said. "Not too crazy about the idea myself. They call the only other alternative desertion, though."

33

TOM AND SARAH huddled together in one corner of the shack where the splintered pine logs that formed the south side met the stark canyon wall that constituted the back. Saddles, deer hides, and supplies were stacked fortress-like about them in an attempt to ward off the wind and snow that whipped through the gaping cracks between the timbers.

When they had returned dazed and exhausted to the canyon camp the previous night, they gathered everything in sight and barricaded the corner as best they could. Then they had stumbled into the little shelter and, pulling blankets over their heads, waited out the storm. The wind had wailed eerily throughout the night, and Tom dozed only sporadically as the numbing, creeping cold aborted his efforts to sustain sleep.

Tom and Sarah had spoken only a few perfunctory words since their harrowing exodus down the trail. Throughout the night, whenever Tom had glanced down at Sarah nestled tightly, almost fearfully, against his shoulder, he could see the whites of her round eyes, almost fluorescent-like in the dark as she stared, unblinkingly, at the wall. Once, he had asked her if she was warm enough, but received no response. It was as if she were lost in another world, oblivious to his presence and to the blizzard that threatened their very lives.

She had evidently suffered a sleepless night, but it was now past noon, and she seemed lost in deep slumber as her head rested against his shoulder. During the crisis on the trail, he had professed his love to this golden-haired enigma; he had blurted out the words like a guileless country bumpkin, and now he felt awkward and embarrassed by it. Would she remember his words? If so, would she laugh them off, make light of the whole thing? No, that was not Sarah's way. On occasion, her sense of humor was needle-like, but in a matter so close to the heart, the sensitive, compassionate Sarah would try to ease rejection's pain. He admitted to himself that he had indeed fallen in love with Sarah, but now his ecstasy was dampened by the realization that his love might not be reciprocated. Uncertainty seized his mind when he looked ahead to the possibility of a separation—perhaps forever—from the bewitching creature beside him.

He looked down at Sarah's pale face, so terribly innocent and vulnerable now in sleep. Her sensuous lips curved ever so slightly upward as though she might be lost in a pleasant dream. Prickly sensations, like spiny cactus needles sticking in his flesh, rippled up and down Tom's arm, and numbness overtook the limb. He wiggled his fingers and made a fist a few times, seeking to stimulate the tired arm, and in doing so, jostled Sarah's head. She shook her head drowsily, and her eyes blinked open.

"I didn't mean to wake you," he said.

"The wind's stopped," she observed matter-of-factly.

"You're a bright girl," Tom said. "It's also afternoon and I'm hungry as a bear." He tossed off the snow-speckled blankets and rose stiffly, extended his hand and pulled Sarah to her feet.

When Tom opened the creaky shack door, the sun struggled to peek through the overcast sky above, and the glare of the clean fresh snow blinded him momentarily. The wind had done some strange things with the snow. In some spots, especially near the creek, gray rock rose nakedly from the earth where the wind had swept, almost polished, its surface clean. A knee-high blanket of white covered much of the canyon floor, however, and along the canyon wall, enormous drifts, many several times Tom's height, curved out like ocean waves rising in a hurricane.

Tom's eyes searched for some sign of the trail. "Sarah," he said, "I can't even make out the trail. Even if I could, I don't know how we'd get out of here. We're trapped . . . just like a couple of rabbits in a snare. We'd just as well get ready for a long stay . . . a hell of a long stay."

"If you'll scare up some wood, I'll fix us something to eat," Sarah replied, and moved back into the cabin. Now she was the pragmatic, practical Sarah.

Tom was relieved to see that she had cast off her dazed stupor. They would have to pull together if they were going to come to the end of this ill-fated trek alive.

Later, as they hunkered by the little fire south of the shack, they attacked hot biscuits and beans like two hungry wolves. After she had devoured her fill, Sarah finally asked, "Tom, you never really explained about Billy. You said he got away from the Indians, but I don't think you told me everything."

Tom related the bits of information he had received from Joe during their hasty flight from the Sioux village. "Joe didn't think Billy could've lived long in those hills, and I've got to say things look pretty bad. I'm sorry, Sarah, but you're going to have to accept the fact that Billy may never be found."

Sarah was silent for a moment. Tom's eyes met hers directly. Against the sculptured white background of the canyon walls, her eyes were ice blue. They were determined eyes, but sensitive, understanding. Damn, he was clay in her hands.

Finally, Sarah said, "Tom, I won't accept the notion that Billy's dead. I can't believe that Stone Dog's death was wasted. Billy's alive somewhere, and we'll find him . . . we have to."

Tom shook his head in disbelief.

For the next week, Tom and Sarah poured themselves into the task of survival. Tom released the horses to forage for themselves in the meager grass and underbrush that grew farther up the canyon. There was no way they could escape, and, with luck, they would survive the winter. The meat supply would be no problem. Rabbit and deer were bountiful throughout the canyon, and the snow cover made tracking easy. Trout flourished in the creek that raced by their camp. The diet might be monotonous, but they would not starve.

The real enemy now was winter. Fortunately, the days had warmed somewhat since the storm. The sun had shone brightly the last three days, and the light thaw that resulted formed a heavy crust on top of the snow discouraging further shifting by the wind.

More importantly, the break in the weather had given Tom and Sarah a last chance to fortify themselves against winter's inevitable attacks.

Tom chiseled hard red clay from the banks farther up the creek, and Sarah warmed the chunks at the fire until they were pliable enough to use for chinking the holes between the timbers. Using the stones that were already in the shack, they rebuilt the crude fireplace. The deerskins harvested in the Black Hills and preserved at Stone Dog's insistence, now provided warming rugs for the cold, stone floor of the shack. A single buffalo hide softened the floor beneath their bedrolls. Excitedly, like newlyweds, Tom and Sarah planned the rustic furniture and other trappings they would fashion for the abode in the weeks to come.

Outside the dwelling, they constructed a series of large windbreaks by piling limbs and branches along the north edge of the camp area, stretching perhaps some twenty feet from the cabin. While weather permitted, Tom amassed huge stacks of firewood just outside the cabin door, and Sarah lashed together long poles with rawhide strips to make frames for stretching animal skins and hanging meat. Nature would provide all of the preservative they would need.

Tonight after they finished supper and just before darkness swallowed the canyon, Tom added another armload of firewood to his growing stacks. He stepped into the shack and moved to the fireplace, stretching his hands over the flickering flame to catch its warm glow. Sarah knelt near the fire, her slender fingers moving smoothly and deftly as she sliced narrow strips of rawhide from buckskin.

Tom watched her silently. The orange firelight cast its luster on her serene face, all of its radiant warmth seeming to focus on this one spot in the otherwise dark, austere room. A crackling fire, a pretty, gentle woman—funny how they seemed to belong together. One without the other, it was not quite the same.

Throughout the entire journey, and especially the past week, he had been awed by her willingness to perform the tough, often punishing, physical tasks ordinarily reserved for the male of the species. She had chopped and carried wood, even hunted game, everything Tom could have expected of a man.

Still, not for one moment, had Tom been unconscious of Sarah's womanliness. He commended himself for the priest-like restraint he had exhibited as she slept beside him during those long, restless nights. But was he really all that virtuous? Indecisiveness had never been a part of his character, but now he found himself uncertain, hesitant. It was unthinkable, with this woman, that he would ever force his affections upon her. Yet he wanted her—wanted her badly—but only if she shared his passion.

Alone these recent days, they had grown to know each other as they never had before. During the day, they found little time to talk; but, at night, sitting cross-legged in front of the fireplace, they talked for hours sharing their family histories, little personal anecdotes, their hopes and dreams—sharing in laughter and sadness. In all of their conversations, however, they had never discussed their feelings for each other. Sarah had not alluded to Tom's acknowledgment of love made that bitter night on the canyon trail, nor did either touch upon other tender moments they had shared together. They skirted this area of their relationship guardedly, and Tom thought, ironically, in spite of all that had passed between them, they might be brother and sister. He wanted more than a sisterly love, but if this was all that it would be, he could accept it—as long as he could be with her.

Tom shivered as he felt a draft gust around his neck. The shack still needed some more work, and the cold was starting to bite at his ears. "Do you suppose it's about time to call it a night?" he said. "It's starting to get nippy."

"Go ahead," she answered, "I'll be along in a minute."

Tom stepped out the door and came back quickly with another armload of firewood, tossing a few of the heavier logs on the dwindling flame. As the logs ignited, orange flames crept higher, warming the shack noticeably. Tom pulled off his boots and slipped under a pile of blankets.

Shortly, Sarah followed suit. He felt the warmth of her body next to his as she snuggled close. Usually, she wanted to talk awhile at this time, but tonight she was strangely quiet. They lay there silently for the better part of a half hour, heads tilted toward the fire's dancing flames, catching its warm glow full on their faces. Sarah lay nearer the fire, only a few feet from its warmth, and Tom could not see her face.

"Tom," she said without turning her head.

"Yes."

"Do you remember the night we came down the canyon trial in the blizzard after we left Joe?"

"My memory's not that short," he teased.

"After my horse went over the side, you said something to me. . . . Do you remember?" she said softly.

"Yes," he said, his voice cracking slightly as he swallowed. "I said 'I love you.'"

"Did you mean it, or were you just saying it?"

"I meant it. . . . I guess more than anything I've ever said."

They both stared uneasily at the fire; Tom's mind grasped for the right words, but they seemed to die in his throat.

After a few moments, Sarah said, "Tom."

"Yes."

"I wonder how many nights we've spent lying next to each other like this over the last three months."

"I don't know," he said, irritation creeping into his voice. "I don't see what difference it makes."

Sarah said, "Ever since that night on the trail, I've been thinking. We don't know if we'll ever get out of here, or if we do, whether we'll ever live to see home again. We've been here alone for a week now, and you never once tried to make love to me. . . . You haven't even tried to kiss me. . . . Don't you want to, Tom?"

"Yes," he said shakily.

She turned toward him, taking his hand in hers, her fingers interlacing his. "Tom, I love you, too. I've never felt anything like this before . . . and I want you to make love to me." She pressed hard against him, and he wrapped his arms around her back; her moist lips met his, and he held her tight, like he was afraid this moment might somehow slip away.

"Oh, Tom," she murmured, her lips against his neck, "you don't know how much I've wanted this . . . wanted you."

"I think I do . . . I think I do, Sarah," he breathed.

She pulled his hand to her breast, and he felt the softness underneath her denim shirt. Then she pulled away for a few moments, and he saw her unbutton the shirt and slip it off before she wormed her way out of her trousers. He followed her example; shortly they lay naked in each other's arms. She stirred and he quickened as her soft skin brushed against his. He thought he could endure no more when she pulled him to her, and he was suddenly lost in the dizzying ecstasy of her body. Their lovemaking was violent and passionate, and they found release quickly. When he withdrew, they lay there together, her head resting on his chest, one leg tossed easily over his thigh. They lay silently until minutes stretched into an hour, neither wanting to break the spell.

Then Sarah said softly, "Tom?"

"Yes."

"Can we do it again?"

He moved to her and they did, this time slowly and gently.

34

JOE LED THE heaving bay mare down Cheyenne's snow-packed main street. The fine-boned animal looked like a docile dog tagging along after the giant who led her, and the sweat that streamed down her flanks, in spite of the cold, showed that she had been ridden to near prostration. It was obviously a case of too little horse for too much man.

When Joe had taken his leave of Fort Fetterman some days earlier, he was forced to accept the only mount the post could spare. Before he rode out of the fort one brisk morning, he told the lieutenant he would be in Cheyenne if his friends showed up, and then pointed the small bay south into the white-patched landscape. The tough, spirited mare gave her best, but Joe found himself walking nearly as much as he rode. The day before he made Cheyenne, a numbing cold spell descended suddenly from the mountains, and in his hurry to escape its wrath, Joe had pushed the mare to her limits.

The sun had been down for several hours now, but the bright moonglow that bounced off the white streets this clear night made it easy to see. Joe had the drawn, hollow look of a tired man as he hobbled down the street, mesmerized by the shimmering kerosene lamps that lined the boardwalks, comforted by the ring of laughter and music rising from the saloons.

He returned to his senses when he bumped into a grizzled old man crossing the street. "Excuse me, mister," Joe said, "guess I was half asleep."

"That's all right, young man," Crawdad Logan answered. "I'm just a bit tipsy right now myself." Then, cocking his head quizzically, he peered more directly at Joe. "For Christ's sake, man, are you all right? You look like hell. . . . And that little mare looks like she's had about all she can handle. Where'd you come from?"

"I feel like I've been through hell . . . or someplace like it," Joe answered. "I've just come down from Fetterman country. A man could freeze his balls off out there these past few days."

"I'd say you need a shot of whiskey down your gullet and some hot beans in your gut. Come on with me over to the Miners Inn," the old man ordered, "they'll put you up for the night." He relieved Joe of the mare's reins. "I'll see to this little gal just as soon as you're settled in."

As they approached the Miners Inn, a rain-warped, two-story building, Joe hesitated. "Mister, I thank you for your kindness, but I'm not sure they'll have room for me in this place."

"Hell, they always got room this time of year," said Crawdad. "Only folks that ain't got sense enough to get out of this country come winter is a bunch of buggy ol' miners. Come on, let's get out of this cold."

Joe was still reluctant. "That's not what I meant. In case you hadn't noticed, some folks would say I'm a Negro and that I'm not welcome there."

"Well, that's nice," grumbled Crawdad. "Most folks would call me a nosey old fart. Being a black man can't be much worse." The old man took Joe by the arm and pulled him through the door of the Miners Inn.

The two men marched up to an unpainted, pine counter and were greeted by an elderly, bespectacled man with a friendly, cherubic face. "Howdy, Crawdad. What can I do for you boys?" the clerk inquired.

"Got a fella here that needs a room," Crawdad said. "He's about frizzed his tonsils off and's plumb tuckered out. Can you fix him up?"

"Sure can. Be a buck in advance, though."

Joe's face relaxed, and his mouth stretched into a relieved smile. Fumbling in his saddlebags, he pulled out a shiny dollar and tossed it on the counter.

The clerk handed him a key. "Room 203. Upstairs and to your left."

Crawdad said, "Tell ya what, mister, you fetch your things up to your room, and I'll tend to your horse. Then you come on down, and we'll go in and have your first drink and meal in Cheyenne on me." Then, to the clerk, "Oscar, in about an hour, this feller's gonna need a hot bath. Why don't you have Billy fill the tub and my friend will be along directly."

Crawdad started to lead Joe back out the door and then stopped. "Oh, by the way," he said extending his rough, gnarled hand, "my handle's Crawdad Logan."

Grasping Crawdad's hand firmly, Joe responded with a broad, warm smile, "My name's Joe Carnes . . . and I'm mighty glad to be in Cheyenne."

35

JOE WALKED DOWN the creaky, splintered steps of the Miners Inn and stepped into the narrow lobby. It was nearly noon and his stomach rumbled hungrily. After his steaming bath the night before, he had climbed the stairs and tumbled into the straw-matted bed, dropping instantly into a dead, exhausted sleep. He had not awakened until an hour earlier, and now his eyes were alive and bright, his manner confident, almost cocky. He greeted the day clerk and then swaggered into the noisy, smoky dining room. He spied Crawdad Logan at a table with a younger companion and strolled in their direction.

"Well," said Crawdad, "I'll be damned if you ain't a different lookin' critter this morning. Last night you was in a hell of a shape."

"I'm fine today," Joe responded, "thanks to you. I'd like you and your friend here to have dinner on me today."

"Sounds like a mighty good deal to me," Crawdad said. "This here's my partner, Jasper Johnson."

Jasper stood and offered his hand. "Howdy," he said. "Welcome to Cheyenne." "Thanks," Joe said. "I like what I've seen so far . . . good food, soft bed, hot bath. It's been a hell of a long time since I've had those comforts."

He pulled a chair up to the table. The men did not need to order; there was only one meal on the menu—beef stew and biscuits, with hot coffee to wash it down. Joe wolfed down three helpings as his guests looked on in awe.

"I hope you can afford that appetite, Joe," Crawdad said. "Cheyenne's a mighty costly place to hole up come winter. Things get short, and prices shoot sky high."

"Well," said Joe, "I've got enough cartwheels stashed away to hold out for a couple of weeks, but no more. It's a long story, but I'm supposed to meet some friends here. We split up back in the mountains with Sioux breathing down our necks just before a storm hit. They were supposed to meet me at Fetterman, but they didn't show up. All I can do is wait it out and see if they make it."

Crawdad shook his head soberly. "Sounds like a miracle you got out of those hills, young feller. I wouldn't count on two miracles. Don't bet on ever seein' your friends again." He saw the gloom spread over Joe's face and moisture glisten in his eyes. "I'm sorry, Joe," the old man said, "I didn't say that right. Those folks must mean somethin' to you."

"Yeah," Joe said, "You might say they're as close to family as I got. There's only one thing, old timer, you don't know those folks. They've got gravel in their gizzards. It may be a spell, but I've got a hunch they're going to show up here one of these days."

"I hope you're right," Crawdad said, "I hope you're right. I tell ya what—looks like you're gonna need work if you stay around here. I happen to know Big Wilma needs a bouncer up to her place, and you sure as hell look like you could handle the job.

You get room and board and a dollar a day . . . not a bad deal."

"Sounds good to me," said Joe. "What is it . . . tavern?"

"Well, uh," Crawdad answered, "some folks call it . . . uh . . . a bawdy house."

"What?" Joe's teeth flashed. "I'm gonna be a bouncer in a whorehouse? Now that does sound interesting . . . mighty interesting."

Crawdad blushed noticeably. "Well, you ain't got the job yet," he grumbled. "I tell ya what, Jasper and me was just goin" up to see Billy. You come along, and we'll put in a good word for you."

"Billy?" Joe asked.

"Yeah," Crawdad said, "that straw-haired little feller that filled your tub last night. Oh, guess you didn't see him; he must have had the tub filled before you got in there. He helps out down here for some extra jangle. The boy's a workin' fool. Miserly little feller, too." Joe was visibly shaken. "What's the matter?" Crawdad asked. "You act like you've seen a ghost."

"No," Joe said, "the name Billy just has a familiar ring to it."

"Well, you'll meet the little guy soon enough. And my guess is he'll take to you like a tick to a hound."

Joe walked with his new friends up the steep, winding road that led to Big Wilma's place, set off like a grand mansion from the other buildings in Cheyenne. The sun shone brightly and a slick glaze formed on the road where the hard-packed snow had thawed just a bit. Joe's eyes were drawn to the filmy outline of the snow-capped mountains to the North.

"What are the chances of getting the kind of warm spell that would open up the mountains before winter really sets in?" he asked?

"You can forget about it till spring," Crawdad said matter-of-factly. "Old Man Winter's just playin' games with us today. You wait and see, a few more days and we'll be froze in here to stay."

Joe turned to the business at hand. "What's this Big Wilma going to think about hiring a black man?" he said, just a trace of anxiety in his tone betraying his concern? "I don't want to make any trouble for you and Jasper."

"Christ's sake," Crawdad answered. "You're really wire-edged about this 'black' business, ain't ya, big feller? Why in the hell should she care if your green or purple, if your man enough to throw the ornery bastards out of her place?"

Jasper, ordinarily quiet, interjected, "Joe, in Cheyenne nobody gives a darn who ya are or what you've done. You've spent some time out west, but I don't think much of it's been in town. Sure we got our bad ones and troublemakers in Cheyenne, but most of us are a bunch of castoffs and ne'er-do-wells chasin' a dream. There's stories about half the guys in this town that would curl your hair, but as long as you got the coin to pay your bills, you'll get along all right with most of the folks around here."

Their boots thumped noisily on Big Wilma's large porch, announcing their arrival even before Crawdad rapped on the heavy, oak door. The dusky Carmella appeared at the door and instantly Joe swept off his hat and smiled. She looked appraisingly up and down his muscular body for a moment and finally her impassive almond-shaped eyes met his. Then she turned to the others. "Hi, Crawdad. Hi, Jasper. Come on in. Your friend, too."

As they stepped onto the thick buffalo hide that covered the foyer, Crawdad said, "This here's Joe Carnes. Joe, this is Carmella. She's one of Big Wilma's . . . Uh . . . girls."

"Pleased to meet you, Carmella," Joe said, his eyes drawn

unavoidably to the mountainous swellings that refused to deny the ample figure beneath the proper, high-necked dress. Then he caught the faintly exasperated look in her sultry eyes and said, "Uh . . . nice place you have here."

Crawdad came to his rescue. "Jasper and me came to see Billy, and the big feller wants to palaver with Big Wilma about the job she's got. What do ya think, Carmella? Looks like he could handle it right well, don't he?"

"Well, I don't know," she teased, "some of these big fellows aren't as tough as they look. I'll bet he'd eat us out of house and home, too."

"Crawdad, you handsome devil," Big Wilma burst into the room. "Billy!" she yelled. "Come on out. Crawdad and Jasper are here."

Billy darted into the big hall and ran up to Crawdad, and a welcoming grin spread across his face. Crawdad tousled his hair affectionately.

"Billy, I want you and Wilma to meet a friend of mine . . . Joe Carnes."

Their eyes turned to Joe who was obviously taken aback, his lips set sober, his eyes narrowing with puzzlement.

"You all right, Joe? What's the matter?" asked Crawdad?

Joe stared at the boy, shaking his head in disbelief. "I know I didn't see this boy last night," he stammered. "If I had, I'd have known him right away. Those damn blue eyes . . . that smile. This has got to be Billy Kesterson."

Stunned silence permeated the room as the others looked at Joe in surprise. Billy broke the silence, "Do I know you, mister?"

"No, but I've been looking for you for better than three months," Joe said. He sighed and turned to Big Wilma. "Do you suppose we could sit down someplace ma'am? I think we've all got a lot to talk about."

"It sure sounds like it," said Big Wilma. "Come on in here. I've got to hear what this is all about." She led the way into her elegant "greeting room." Then, sinking into a soft, overstuffed chair, Joe related his story, Billy interrupting frequently to fill in the gaps from his own perspective.

Finally, Joe finished. "I guess that's about it. I last saw Tom and Sarah heading southeast back toward the canyon. I don't know if they ever made it. . . . If they did, I don't know when or how they'll ever get out. We shouldn't have ever separated. Anyhow, it looks like I'm stuck here till spring. If they don't show up soon after the first good thaw, I'll head back up there and try to find out what happened."

Crawdad said, "I panned gold up that way before I went into the Black Hills. You must've been in what the miners call Roaring Canyon. That shack you mentioned sure sounds like it. If they got back there before the blizzard and got sense enough to stay put, they might have a chance."

"Anyway, Joe," Big Wilma interjected, "you've got yourself a job if you want it."

"Thanks," said Joe. "I want it."

36

JOE STAYED THE winter in Cheyenne sharing Billy's room at Big Wilma's, and, welded closer by their common loss, he and the boy became fast friends. Noise and laughter shook the gracious mansion at nights, but during the cold winter afternoons, a lazy peaceful atmosphere settled in. Crawdad and Jasper made it a part of their daily ritual to drop by Big Wilma's and spend the afternoons with Joe, swapping stories near the warm fireside. Billy and Big Wilma joined the little group frequently, and, as winter faded slowly into spring, Carmella found her way into the room with increasing regularity.

Whenever Carmella was in the room, Crawdad was pleased to assume the burden of carrying the conversation as Joe turned silent, obviously distracted by the presence of Carmella's dark beauty. His eyes followed her every move, and his brow wrinkled in bewilderment when she entered into the friendly discourse, always exhibiting a sharp, inquisitive mind and keen intellect that belied her sensuous, seductive eyes.

One day, when they sat alone at the kitchen table, Joe said, "Carmella, I'm puzzled. You just don't seem to be the kind of person that would fit into this . . . uh . . . business."

"You mean, what's a nice girl like me doing in a place like this?" she said sarcastically. "I've heard that line before, mister. Let me just say this: I've got to eat, and I'm saving every cent I make. I'm not going to spend the rest of my life doing this. I've got plans. One more year and that's it. And in case you've got any ideas, just remember . . . no free samples."

Hurt shadowed Joe's eyes. "I'm sorry, Carmella, I didn't mean to upset you. I was just interested. I really do care."

Carmella's eyes softened and a light mist blurred their clearness. "I'm the one who should be sorry, Joe. I know you didn't mean any harm." She reached across the table and took his huge hand in hers. "You're a special kind of man. I've just become too tough and hard. I do want you to understand one thing, though. As hard as it may be, this is just a business with me—just the same as a storekeeper selling his goods or a farmer working his ground. It's a long story, but I learned that I could make my way real well doing what I'm doing. I don't like it, but it's a way to get where I want to go. And Joe, you'll never be a customer of mine; I don't want it to be that way between us. Let's just let things ride awhile and see what happens. If you can accept what I am, and if there's to be something more for us, I think we'll both know when the time's right."

"All right, Carmella," Joe said. "We'll at least have time to see what happens. I've got to find out about Tom and Sarah, but no matter what, I'll be sticking around these parts. I've got some plans that will keep me here . . . at least in the winters. Maybe I can convince you that you don't need your job another year. If I can't, I'll be here when that year's up."

Carmella was one of the several reasons why Joe had decided

not to return to Nebraska. His friend, Crawdad Logan, had made him an offer Joe was going to take up. Crawdad insisted he had marked a spot in the Black Hills where a gold find was a sure thing. It was well beneath the granite surface, and the unsettled times in the hills had made it impossible for him to stay and pursue his hunch. Crawdad maintained that the government would open the Black Hills to civilians again soon, and everything pointed to a big military campaign against the Sioux in the spring. It would not be long before they could return and stake a claim.

Crawdad could still pan for gold, but mining the hard rock was another thing. He had the mining know-how, but he needed somebody with some business sense and a couple of big, young bulls to do the work. Joe fit the bill on both counts. Crawdad and Jasper proposed to cut Joe in as a one-third partner if he would go to the hills in the spring to help work the claim. It had taken Joe about half a minute to say yes.

"If Billy's sister and the young man ain't showed up come spring," said Crawdad, "we'll take Billy with us. We'll try to find out what happened to them on the way."

37

APRIL'S WARMING BREEZES caressed the frosty mountain tops now, and the icy creeks and streams that snaked through the foothills north and west of Cheyenne raced bank-full through the rocky gorges and canyons as the white blanket shrank from the ground. A few miles to the North, two riders forded a little creek, swollen and raging from the thaw brought on by the bright spring sun. Tom's horse followed Sarah's onto the solid footing offered by the rocky creek bank, and they dismounted, Tom pulling steadily at the lead rope of the string of heavy-laden pack horses as they splashed through the stream and clambered from the chilling, foamy waters.

"We'll be in Cheyenne inside an hour," Tom said. "If the C. O. at Fetterman was right, Joe ought to be there." He wrapped his arm around Sarah's shoulders and pulled her close. "Sarah, after we find Joe, we'll head up to the Black Hills and have another go at finding Billy . . . if that's what you want."

Sarah shook her head negatively, her clear eyes meeting Tom's. "No, there comes a time to go on. I think this is it. I want to go home. If Billy's dead, there's nothing we can do. If he somehow got back to our people, he'll find a way to get home, or somebody will be in touch."

She spoke matter-of-factly. Tom knew she had come to terms with her grief and was ready now to make a new life. After their winter in the mountains, Tom no longer doubted they would share the future.

He pulled her chin up gently and planted a soft kiss on the tip of her nose. "You kind of grow on a fella, you know that? I could get used to having you around."

"You darn well better say that, Captain Carnes," Sarah said mysteriously.

"What do you mean by that?"

Deliberately ignoring his query, Sarah moved to her horse. "Let's head for Cheyenne," she said.

Later, as they walked their horses up Cheyenne's sloppy, muddy main street, Tom observed that the town was alive and jumping with miners, packing and getting ready to move north into the mountains. He sidled his horse over to the hitching post in front of a busy general store hailing a stocky, congenial-looking miner. "I'm looking for a man by the name of Joe Carnes. Ever heard of him?"

"Sure enough," the miner answered. "He's a partner of Crawdad Logan's. You ought to find him at Big Wilma's." He pointed to the big white house perched alone on a hillside some distance up the street.

Tom turned to Sarah and grinned. "Sounds like Joe's been busy."

Sarah smiled back. Then turning again to the miner, Tom asked, "Is there a preacher in this town?"

The man looked at Sarah and beamed. "You bet. It's been a

long spell since he's done anything but funerals, and he'd be mighty proud to see you. Let's see . . . this time of day, he's likely in Harley's Saloon."

"Thanks much, friend," Tom said and reined his horse up the street without so much as a glance at Sarah. Sarah did not follow.

Shortly, Tom wheeled his horse around and trotted the animal back to Sarah. "Aren't you coming?" he asked.

"Well, I might . . . if I take the notion." Her blue eyes twinkled. "What's this business about the preacher? Were you trying to tell me something a little bit ago?" she asked.

"That was a proposal, ma'am," he said sheepishly.

"Tom Carnes. You're supposed to be a sophisticated, educated man. If you can't do better than that, you'll never find a wife."

He knew she was having her fun, but he guessed he had not handled this too gracefully. She deserved better.

He sat straight in his saddle and swept off his wide-brimmed hat. "Miss Kesterson," he said, "would you do me the honor of giving me your hand in marriage?"

"Well, I'll think about it," she teased. She rubbed her chin and bit her lips, narrowing her eyes as though in deep and troubled thought. Abruptly she said, "I've thought about it. . . . I accept. Besides, I think it would be nice for Samuel Kesterson Carnes to have a father."

Taken aback, Tom said, "Do you mean—"

"I'm trying to tell you something." She laughed. She edged her horse next to his, leaned over, and kissed him warmly on the cheek.

"Let's go find Joe," he said. "Then, we'll get the preacher. Then we're heading home to the Double C."

"Double C . . . and Big K," she corrected. "Don't forget, we've got the Kesterson ranch to run, too."

"I don't imagine you'll let me forget," he said.

As they drew near the big white house, Tom could make out a giant dark man standing on the wide, front porch engaged in an animated conversation with a blond-haired little boy.

"Joe!" he yelled, waving excitedly.

As Tom nudged his horse ahead, Joe looked up and grinned. He said something to the little boy and stepped off the porch, striding rapidly toward the riders. The boy darted past Joe, almost knocking him over as he pushed by and raced down the road, tears streaming from his blue eyes as he raced toward the golden-haired lady on the horse.

Made in the USA
San Bernardino, CA
07 March 2016